All Is Now Lost

A cozy mystery rooted in the
South Carolina Lowcountry

Laura Elizabeth

For more information and to get to know the author, visit:
TheIslandMysteries.com

Cover design by Rick Nease
RickNeaseArt.com

Published by Front Edge Mystery, an imprint of Front Edge Publishing.

Do you have a mystery you'd love to share with the world? For more information about publishing with Front Edge, please visit FrontEdgePublishing.com or contact info@ FrontEdgePublishing.com.

Front Edge Publishing, LLC
42807 Ford Road
Canton, MI
48162

Front Edge Publishing books are available for discount bulk purchases for events, corporate use and small groups. Special editions, including books with corporate logos, personalized covers and customized interiors are available for purchase. For more information, contact Front Edge Publishing at info@FrontEdgePublishing.com

To Jay, Meghan, and Colin

Our walks on the beach, hours spent exploring our island, early evening jaunts, tidbits on screened porches, game nights, and the many ways we found to enjoy our time together all helped me create this story. I am eternally grateful for all these wonderful memories and our grand adventures yet to come. Thank you for your love, support, and for sharing my belief in island magic.

Chapter 1

"So ... this is our new island hot spot, I hear," someone called from the doorway of Books & Brew, the bookstore I had just opened. I was in the far back corner, polishing the tall oak shelves, trying to bring out their natural patina. Instantly I realized I had forgotten to lock the door behind me when arriving earlier.

"Hello?" I answered, trying to decide my next move. I was in it now. I stood and started to move slowly toward the front of the store.

"Just want to welcome you to the neighborhood, so to speak. Say hello and all that. Should I come back?" In the front room stood a tall man with what seemed like a perpetual tan. He was wearing a roomy gray sweatshirt with the Black Dog logo across the front. His jeans were worn and faded. He looked casual, comfortable, and relaxed, with both hands tucked into his front pockets.

Picking up the pace, I smiled and greeted him quickly, "No, please come in. It's so nice to meet you. I am Carr Jepson, thanks for popping in. I am sorry to say there isn't much to see yet. I am just getting started, really."

"Carl Tibbons, pleasure. Welcome, it's great to see some new life on our main street," he said as his large hand swallowed mine in a firm shake.

"When are you expecting to open? I bet you want to be ready before the busy season, right?" Carl asked. "When the tourists come, it is everybody's busy season, that's for sure, even mine."

I nodded as he spoke, "Yes, that's exactly what I am hoping for. The inventory and all the pieces will fall into place for the busy season. I want to hit the ground running."

"How'd you land on Mongin Island? This place is a pretty well-kept secret. How'd you stumble upon our quirky little hideaway?"

I smiled at him, "You're right about that! My family came here for a vacation fifteen years ago, on a whim really. No one we knew had ever seen or heard of this place but the seed was planted for me when I read a magazine story about a month or so before our trip. I was intrigued. The pictures sold it and the family was up for the challenge of trying a new place. It was love at first sight, I guess you might say." He nodded vaguely as if he had heard this story or a version of it many times before. "A magazine, you say? Interesting."

I paused, deciding how much to share before continuing, "We purchased a home on the Rosemont resort property and have been vacationing here, a few weeks at a time, for years. But I only moved here full time recently and well, one day last month Barb Hawkins and I bumped into Allen as he was packing up his T-shirt store. The rest I guess you could say, is history. Can I make you a cup of tea? Please, come in and sit for a minute."

Carl smiled kindly, removed his fishing hat and replied, "Sure I'm not interrupting you?"

I could already tell he wanted to know more about what was happening here, and I knew enough about island culture to know we were having tea and talking, no matter what else I had been working on or what I had previously planned to do.

"I insist," I said. "Please make yourself comfortable. Well, as comfortable as you can in those straight back chairs. Be back in a bit!"

In just a few minutes, we were settled at the long farm table in the back room, sharing our collective list of the benefits of living on Mongin Island. We agreed on quite a few things right away. The idea that there were hardly any cars on the island, there were no busy roads, no crowds, no traffic lights, no bridge, these were all things we appreciated.

Carl shared that he lived in the lighthouse and ran the museum housed in the front room there. "It's not really a working lighthouse, as you likely already know. I mean, it has a light and all, but it's just a matter of flipping a switch at night. The lighthouse is not really helping much from its current location. I like to say it's more of a tradition than a function. Years ago, I knew I needed more to keep me busy. It's been at least twenty years, maybe more, that I have been working on selling properties here on the island and a little on the mainland, too. You know how it is here, there aren't that many of us to go around. Heck, I am not the only one who wears multiple hats. We all do a little of everything. That's how we make it all work here, I guess.

"I suppose I never bumped into you since the property you purchased is part of the resort," he said. "People tend to check into the Inn and if they catch 'island fever' they often look first at the properties they can see from their hotel room or a restaurant or whatever. You know, the resort has their own realtors that sell the lots and homes there and that's fine. It leaves the other seven miles of the island for me!" he laughed.

"It's funny you say that, because that's exactly what happened to us," I said. "We stayed at the Inn, experienced 'resort life' and really didn't explore much beyond there. The resort had everything we needed and wanted in a second property. The house we looked at was perfect; we made the deal. We all love the resort amenities, the golf, the tennis, the horseback riding, the restaurants, and even the spa. To have all of that within walking distance of our home worked for us then and it certainly works well for me now. It is really nice to be new to the island as a full time resident and have a built-in neighborhood and social life. Everyone has been really welcoming, actually."

We spent a few more minutes chatting about island life, then Carl looked down at his watch. "Heavens, apologies, I've kept you long enough. I know you have a lot on your plate right now. Setting up a new business can be a challenge." He stood up quickly, grabbed his empty mug and walked familiarly to the little kitchenette Allen had installed years ago, when this shop was the T-Shirt Gallery. Clearly, Carl had been here many times before and likely knew this store better than I did. I smiled but said nothing.

As he moved away from the sink, he said, "Tell me what you plan to do with the room we were just in. I imagine building an inventory is no easy task, especially just getting started and all. Allen used to share a meal with his customers, or sometimes use that table to design a new shirt. Although it really didn't suit him well, he liked this store. He liked watching the golf carts come and go. It's a great location, so close to the ferry landing and all. What are you thinking about for that room?"

I was immediately curious. Was he going to offer some kind of joint venture? Did he know someone who maybe wanted to share this space with me? I could tell Carl had his finger on the pulse of this island and he would be a good ally.

So, I told him a bit of my story. "Actually, the idea of this store has been something on my heart for a long time, I just didn't realize it was there until this opportunity presented itself when we bumped into Allen as he cleared out. This whole venture came as a surprise to me, really. It was like suddenly I had the time, the means, and a place to bring it to life. In my mind, I've always envisioned a store where customers are welcome to come in, find a new book, visit with others, make new friends, discuss books, and get to know people. Basically, I imagined it to be a place that serves as a gathering spot and happens to sell books."

He seemed interested, so I continued, "Here on this island, there isn't a place for books that we have read—and know that a neighbor may enjoy. On the mainland, I could always donate used books to a library, but we can't do that here. So, I was thinking the room we were just in would be a room we would use for book trades. You bring one, you can take one, that kind of thing. This way everyone can still 'shop' at Books & Brew—everyone can be and will be welcome here. That big table is perfect for events or people could just gather around it. You know us Southerners enjoy sharing a meal together, breaking bread together. I want customers to make it their own."

Carl started to say something and then paused. He looked at me deeply. It could have been the first time he really saw me. Quietly, he said, "Amazing, what a clever idea. I love it. Might not make you much money, but definitely will make you rich."

We walked together to the wood and glass front door, where he paused. "Not sure if this is helpful and it's okay to say no, but I have boxes and boxes of pre-loved books. I mean, when I say boxes, I am thinking of multiple dozens of boxes. It is not unusual for people to leave books when they move. Getting stuff off this island is a challenge, and it is expensive to barge everything back and forth. Lots of times we find a box or two in someone's attic or in the back of a closet. You know, as the realtor, sometimes little things like clutter can be a deal breaker, so I always just remove stuff like this before the final walk-through. It kind of keeps the deal going. I sort the boxes as I get them, and get rid of the relics and oddball things. I've always intended to bring a box or bag to the mainland library when they are having their book sale. Never got there and have just been stacking them in my back bedroom. I would be most pleased to donate them to your room. All you have to do is say the word. They will be yours."

I am not sure why, even after my time on the island, this generous act still surprised me. "Carl, that would be truly incredible. Are you sure? That would be a game changer for us. I really didn't want to open the store with an empty room. I have some books of my own I can donate, but honestly, I have a hard time parting with the ones I read to my children."

"Then consider it done, just come by whenever it works for you. You can take what you want—and I can help you move them. I could throw a box or two in my cart and just drop off a box here and there. You know, I live in the rooms behind the museum, at the base of the lighthouse. Just come around the back path, my door is usually unlocked, like most islanders. If I am not there, you can help yourself." He smiled, put his hat back on and walked quickly to his cart. "See you soon and great to meet you."

I didn't miss the gentle nudge that islanders don't lock their doors—they don't keep people out. We welcome people in, we share what we have, we rely on each other to live here often without a built-in network. Full-time residents are a small community. We need each other, for better or worse. We know our neighbors. This isn't some nameless place with nameless people. The resort provided a steady stream of visitors at the Inn. But the residents were the backbone of island life. There were a lot of lessons in Carl's casual visit.

"Carl, thank you so much. Thanks for stopping by and for the books. I would love for you to catch up with Tripp. He is helping me set up and we will be working together once the shop opens. He will be so excited to learn about your donation! Please come back again soon!" I smiled and waved as he turned his cart around and waved over his shoulder. I had a lot to learn about living in this place I loved.

Chapter 2

I will always remember those early days of beginning again with mixed emotions. I awoke each morning intending to be hopeful. I wanted to believe that Mongin Island would heal me and that I would find the peace I so desperately needed—but I was also afraid that even Mongin would not be enough.

Just a few months ago, on a sunless October morning, I boarded the early Mongin Island Ferry with the determination of making my new home on this island off South Carolina's coast. That day, I was too nervous and numb to even think of sitting during that ride, so I stood on deck and grasped the railing with an anxiety I had never felt in crossing these waters with my husband Rob and our kids. We had come to think of Mongin as our island.

That October morning, I was alone and flooded with grief. The engine churned and the ferry rolled into a briny morning fog so thick that I could not even glimpse Mongin until we were almost to the dock. That arrival certainly was not what Rob and I had envisioned as we made our plans to leave behind our large, comfortable house in Atlanta where we had raised our kids and sent them off into the world. We were dreaming of a romantic, new, second life on this island with such a storied past that historians and novelists had chronicled its chapters and filmmakers had shot movies along its shores and its giant, mossy 400-year-old live oaks.

For many years, Rob and I had planned for this milestone: the end of childrearing, hectic family schedules, and the guardrails that kept all the energy of our growing family hemmed into our neat, suburban life—and the beginning of our next stage, together. We envisioned this move happening when our kids were well established and we were young and healthy enough to live on an island without a bridge, hours away from them. The kids were supposed to have their independent lives and we would have ours. Of course, we would all get together for long weekends, trips to the beach, vacations, and holidays and build those bonds with our now adult children and the people our children brought into our lives. This was what today was supposed to be—this end and this beginning. This was how the big move was supposed to unfold, with eagerly anticipated roles for everyone as we built our future together.

This long-term planning included years of intensive professional hurdles that both Rob and I had to clear. Then, we would scale back so we could become year-round islanders with our fingers left in a few carefully chosen professional projects that did not depend on our location. We could play as much golf and pickleball as we wanted—like many of the islanders we had met in our frequent visits to the house we had bought on Mongin. We could catch up on all the reading we'd never done, enjoy home cooking with the rich bounty of coastal ingredients, explore those talents we'd never had time to fully hone and perhaps discover new ones, walk on the beach, and enjoy the fruits of our corporate careers. As Meredith, our oldest, landed her teaching position at a prestigious Atlanta private school and Nicholas, our youngest, graduated from college, the time was nearing for our big move.

Then, on one unseasonably cold morning in April, I woke up and Rob did not. His massive heart attack came as a complete surprise to everyone because he took excellent care of himself. He was the picture of health—a traumatic lesson that things may not be all they seem. I can barely recall the details of the funeral and those first weeks of grief. Days were just a blend of getting through things, too numb and too lost to focus on any one thing.

By May, however, friends and colleagues either assumed that grief had run its course or they simply ran out of things to say. So, they turned to well-intentioned but jarring encouragement that I "get it together as you always do." How could I do that without Rob? The truth was that I was relieved to let our attorney settle all of Rob's affairs for me because it was all I could do to wake up each morning, climb out of bed, and get dressed for the day. Some days, even that didn't happen. As a partner in my consulting firm, each day at work felt like slogging through another marathon of details I could not seem to embrace or internalize.

June, July, and August passed with much of the same: Endless days of me trying to grasp daily life and sorting the many details of starting over again. Even learning to cook for just one and learning to eat in silence without someone to share the tidbits of life felt impossible some days. I was trying to remember how to do all of it. I wanted to be present for my children, who were also dealing with a tremendous loss. Rob had been an exceptional father and I know during this time, they likely felt like they lost us both.

One routine that helped bring consistency and structure to my days was journaling. I committed to writing at least a sentence or two daily. More and more the entries referred to a memory or a thought of Mongin. One day, I finally found a phrase to describe the island's allure: tranquil energy. The same day I jotted that phrase in my journal, I resolved to sell my Atlanta house along with nearly all of its contents, downsize my consulting role to a few projects of my choosing—and to begin a new life on Mongin.

Alone.

Some steps proved easier than others. When I started what I assumed would be a very difficult talk with my business partner, I soon realized he supported my decision to step away.

I was relieved by his first words after I had spilled what I thought was a revelation about my decision to leave: "You know," he said, "I never would have said anything, but—" I was thankful at how

smoothly we developed a plan for the business that would let him
launch a new version of the company, let me recoup, and ensure that I
could still play a small role in the future as long as I wanted to pursue
a few projects. Like me, he was ready to head in a new direction.

Although I presented them with another loss for which they may
not have been completely ready, my children stood with me in this
decision.

"I'm glad you've found the next chapter of your story, Mom,"
Nicholas said at the end of a video call. I could see tears on his
cheeks—and that boy never cried. Those tears were for me, for him,
for us, for all we had lost and for maybe also for what he hoped we
would gain.

"Hey, let's not forget all the wonderful things we had and let's look
forward to the new, wonderful things we will have. We are lucky, still,
to have each other and I am grateful to you and Meredith for having
the strength I did not," I told him, not really feeling the confidence
and enthusiasm I tried to inject into my voice. Still, I wanted him to
be reassured and comforted.

"Mom, don't worry. Believe me, I am grateful. Life is different now
and I get it. Now, realizing home will not be Atlanta anymore, it will
be Mongin, it's just been a lot for all of us," he said softly. "We love
you."

Then, the next morning, with a final wave to our neighbors, I set
out on the four-hour drive to the ferry. Inevitably, I thought of how
far back this journey had started.

When we traveled to Mongin Island fifteen years ago, we had no
idea what we were doing. A year before, Rob's business partnership
had uprooted our idyllic life in Connecticut and transplanted us to
Atlanta. We all felt like ships bobbing on the water with no land in
sight. For Rob, maybe it was a little easier. His law firm asked him to
move and open a new health care law practice as their newest branch.
Rob had a purpose and a promotion. He welcomed the adventure of
carving out a whole new role, networking, and building a business.

Nicholas was in early elementary school and the impact of the
move from the cozy New England suburb was soothed by a great

soccer team and a neighborhood filled with playmates his age who shared his same interests in pick-up sports games, riding bikes, and exploring. Of course, there were times he missed the familiar things—his best buddy, sledding in the winter, the big cedar playscape in the backyard, hot chocolate on a snowy deck, and his favorite places in town. Secure and steady as he was, though, Rob and I were amazed at how fast those things became distant memories. He dove into second grade with confidence, and we only saw an occasional tinge of homesickness that came when things didn't work out so smoothly in his new life. His kind heart, sense of humor, and calm demeanor made him a solid friend among his new buddies and instantly part of the group.

Meredith, on the other hand, hated our new life and everything about it. Change had always been hard for her, and she grew up needing time built into her day to ease the many inevitable transitions of childhood. So, moving to a whole new part of the country and finding friends was tougher for her than it was for Nicholas. At first, we had many long discussions around the kitchen table, punctuated by tears, and Rob and I often wondered if we would ever get our sunny and sweet girl back. She has always been smart with a defined sense of right and wrong. Her strong spirit, incredible curiosity, and sense of adventure were infectious. At home, she would be up for anything and light up the room—but outside, her world was filled with teenage judgment and insecurity. Her first few years in Atlanta were hard, and it was painful to watch, knowing she was unhappy.

From my perspective, I felt extraordinarily lucky to be a partner in a consulting firm that allowed me to take my work with me, especially as digital communication was rapidly expanding. When I told my partner about my plans for the move, he also pointed out that Atlanta was one of the country's most convenient hubs for business travelers. He predicted that, like Rob, I soon would be developing new clients for our firm. Rather than any anxiety about the move, I felt as if I had won the lottery. As the years went on, all of those assumptions proved to be true. Our company's bottom line grew substantially and we considered bringing another partner on board.

Aside from some occasional trips, I was able to work from home at a time when my children needed consistency and a parental presence.

This brings me back to that initial trip to Mongin Island on our first spring break after moving to Atlanta. New to the South, we wanted to explore some of the wonders around us and considered several of the many options the region presented. But Rob and I wanted a place where the kids could freely run around and we all could enjoy family adventures without crowds or long lines. Then, I took a one-day business trip to Savannah and, on a coffee table in the client's lobby, I saw a photo taken just as dawn was breaking along an Atlantic shore with an old lighthouse in near silhouette, outlined by streaks of pre-dawn gold and salmon. An empty beach filled with powdery sand was in the foreground.

I picked up the magazine, a regional quarterly called *South Carolina Shores*, and there was Mongin in all its glory. The story was headlined "Dawn Wakes Up a Sleepy Southern Gem." It was all about how the nation's booming real estate market had hit little Mongin Island and featured a full-page photo of a gloriously oak-lined road, plus splashy photos of the recently expanded resort that featured a sixty-room inn and details of the plan to merge "a timeless history of hospitality with modern amenities." There was even a photo of an oak-and-glass case housed in the island's lighthouse museum. In the case, I could see some old bottles, clay cookware, and a spectacular looking dinner plate believed to be dated to the 1700s. "This island is so steeped in history, you just have to set foot on our miles of beautiful shoreline to start your own adventure," the writer boasted.

My mind was racing. I could picture our kids running along that shoreline.

"How about some beachcombing on an island in the Atlantic?" That was all I said at dinner the following evening before unfolding the magazine I had swiped from my client's lobby. I flipped the pages silently. Nicholas saw that final photo of the shiny treasures in the museum's display case and, suddenly, all four of us were eagerly awaiting a week on Mongin.

Within days, the computer in our family room was full of book-marked links to Mongin and that part of the Atlantic coast. We all found images we loved: beautiful beaches, marshes with tall beach grasses, palm trees, and a historic mansion converted to a hotel called the Rosemont Inn. We were ready! Rob and I reserved spots in a few planned activities each day from the resort's listed amenities, but we kept those from the children, thinking they would enjoy a new surprise each day. This truly would be an adventure of a lifetime. We stuffed the car with suitcases, beach toys, games and golf clubs—and we were off!

We trudged along. As the stops for traffic, food, and breaks piled up, we began to worry about making our reservation on the ferry to the island. Our grand adventure started a little rocky. Tempers frayed. We were hot and tired—and not at all in vacation mode when we pulled into the Mongin Island embarkation station on the tip of South Carolina. With only a few moments to spare, we raced to make the ferry. When we finally stood on the deck, Rob looked at me over the heads of the children and I could tell we were sharing the same thought at that minute: "Maybe *now* is when our grand adventure begins."

While living in New England, we had many previous ferry rides from Hyannis to Nantucket and always said our vacation began when our feet left the dock. On those ferries, three hours of salty sprays on your lips and skin and warm sun on your head made it easy to get lulled into a vacation mindset. This ferry to Mongin, how-ever, was fast. It seemed we barely got settled before we spotted some dolphins racing along with our boat and Mongin Island in our sight line. I hadn't had enough ferry time to fully unwind from the hectic afternoon race toward the docks. Vacation still seemed to elude me.

We moved quickly with the other passengers to the green and white restored trolley waiting for us at the end of the dock. While the bell captains secured all our suitcases and supplies, we boarded and were transported to the resort. I sat on this trolley, thinking about the day we already had—loading the car, the long ride to the ferry, the boat ride, and now this trolley trip, and marveled at how well the kids had both handled it all so far. Something positive was in the air. As we meandered down the main island road, ever so slowly I began to start relaxing the grip I had on my bags and my shoulders started to slide back into their normal position. The air was heavy with humidity, but the palm fronds waved gently as the breeze cooled us down and before I knew it, we were entering the main gate of the resort.

As the trolley turned left into the resort driveway, I realized, in the most unexpected way, that I was home. This place, this magical and mysterious place, was what I had unknowingly been looking for all my life. Through all the places I traveled, I never had experienced any sensation like this. Having never been to this region, all the sights, sounds, and smells were new. It was like having all my senses electrically charged while concurrently feeling like this was the very place I was always meant to be. I was just finding it now for the very first time at thirty-nine years old.

From this point on, we described our life as before Mongin Island, or after Mongin Island.

The stately Rosemont Inn welcomed us with southern hospitality. Seeing its grandeur rise from the lush grounds was breathtaking. The huge front porch ran almost the length of the building and white rockers strategically placed there invited us to enter the large solid oak front door. The Inn was the former mansion of wealthy plantation owners who lived on Mongin Island more than one hundred years ago. Cotton, indigo, and oysters were the main assets the land and the sea produced. The last family descendants sold this property to a boutique hospitality company about ten years before we first visited. They transformed the 400-acre property into a thriving resort, complete with golf, tennis, horseback riding, a spa, and fitness activities. They also added two wings of guest rooms and structurally made changes that accommodated large crowds while keeping the magnificent main rooms and elegant curved grand staircases as the heart of this home.

The week was wonderful. Each day, the island's enchantment grew and grew until, one morning, Rob and I walked into the resort's real estate office and asked to see a yellow house for sale on Captain

Madison Lane. The decision was made before we even got through the whole tour. This house was our perfect paradise home. We were under contract before we arrived back in Atlanta.

Over the years, we enjoyed many other just-as-wonderful vacations at our Mongin home, which we dubbed *La Vida Pacifica*, or "peaceful life." We met our neighbors and were often introduced to visitors, but we did not spend enough consistent time on the island to form deep friendships. That was all supposed to happen when Rob and I moved here full-time together.

So, there I was, alone on this ferry, hoping that Mongin Island still held some magic for me after the trauma of Rob's death. Somehow, I hoped, I might still find a peaceful life.

I braced myself for the little jolt when the ferry bumped the dock. Ropes were thrown. The ramp boomed into place. And finally, my feet touched the dock. I only had a couple of bags to lug along with me. The moving van I had hired to haul some essential furniture and boxes was on its way to the barge dock and would arrive at *La Vida Pacifica* tomorrow.

I looked up at the sky and I could feel Rob cheering me on. These days, all decisions—from simply choosing a cup for coffee to packing my suitcases—were hard. All day long, month after month, nothing had felt right—until this moment.

I was surprised to hear my own voice. I just couldn't help but say it out loud: "I'm home."

Chapter 3

When the van arrived, arranging the furniture and unpacking the boxes I brought with me did not take long—and I was able to settle into a routine. Island life definitely has a rhythm, and I was slowly getting used to it. It was hard to give up the idea of having a structured day and to just have hour after hour to do whatever I wanted. What did I want to do? I didn't even know. Shouldn't I be doing—something? Sure, it was great to go on long walks in the mild winter weather, meet new friends, begin to build relationships with the islanders, read, and practice yoga. All of that was all wonderfully relaxing. But how much more relaxed could I be?

I began to realize that I needed more.

On one of my walks, I bumped into Barb, who was heading to the General Store, the lone place on our island to pick up supplies. You could find one or two of almost anything in this wood-framed shop with wide planked floors and old iron gooseneck light fixtures lining the walls. The ceiling fan was always on, but it never felt like it did much, with the screen door opening and closing all day long. From canned goods to phone chargers and shampoo to produce, you never really knew what you might find. It was a place most islanders visited a few times a week to supplement our more regular shopping on the mainland.

Barb's golf cart was filled with the boxes she was bringing to some of the properties she managed and some extra food she would deliver to the feral cat house someone had constructed near the community farm. Barb and I were about the same size and we both had to sit on the edge of the cart's bench seat to reach the brake. Her face was framed with short blonde hair, her bangs lining her forehead. She wore no make-up, no jewelry, and lived in either Keds sneakers or flip-flops and a variety of cargo shorts, T-shirts, and hoodie sweatshirts. Barb had quite a T-shirt collection, many of which were given to her by visitors who sent her thank-you gifts from their hometowns or colleges. She was unfussy, uncomplicated, and ready at a moment's notice to jump into whatever task was in front of her.

"Hop in," she invited. As I settled into her cart with her, she quickly listed all of her planned errands as if I might want to accompany her. Since moving to the island full-time, Barb had become a great friend and companion. She quit corporate life decades ago and owned several rental properties. Her cottage was on the other side of the resort and we first met one day as she walked a few dogs on long leashes. I immediately liked her as I learned how much we shared: a love of animals, independence, and a no-nonsense approach to life. I also discovered that Barb was a force in island life. Our friendship gave me a quiet confidence and I was immediately comfortable with her and her many adventures.

At the end of her meandering list of errands, she added, "And most important of all—I need to get some of that pie Miss Lucy baked. It's Tuesday and you know they will go fast!"

I didn't need to be asked twice. Miss Lucy's pies were well known on the island and already were a highlight of my own weekly schedule. If we were lucky, we would beat the crowd.

Miss Lucy had lived her whole life on this island, like several generations of her family before her. She rarely left Mongin, and often liked to say she didn't trust land that wasn't sprinkled with sunshine, salt water, and sand. Because Miss Lucy had no desire to be anywhere else, she wasn't interested in what was happening in "big cities with lots of strangers surrounded by concrete." She was as in tune with the island and its residents as the gentle breezes that rustled through the trees lining our roads. She often knew what we needed before we did and she showed her love of our island through the goodness of her pies. Although she might be asking you what you needed, what you wanted, what you thought, she already knew. Her weekly pie specials usually came as a result of a conversation she had with someone on the island. Someone may need a little taste of their own family recipe, a reminder of home, or to celebrate seasonal bounties. Miss Lucy and her pies were an island treasure.

As we neared the gravel lot of the General Store, Barb whooped. "Would you look at that? Miss Lucy is just pulling away! Carr, today is our lucky day! We'll have our first pick of her pies!"

Following her up the wooden stairs, I made a silent promise to try a little harder to incorporate Barb's joy at such simple things. I thought: Maybe she is right. Maybe today is our lucky day.

The line at the register had already formed, but we knew we would not be leaving empty handed today! "Good morning, y'all!" Barb called out to no one in particular as we pulled open the door. You could immediately tell it was Tuesday by the sweet scent of brown sugar and cinnamon in the air. A minute ago, I would have told you I was not at all hungry, but now my stomach was grumbling. Miss Lucy's pies were that good.

"Morning ladies!" Hetty, the store's owner and manager, was ringing up the customer standing in front of her. Greetings with neighbors were exchanged, along with general chit chat about the weather and the newly revised ferry schedule. In a few minutes, it was our turn and the small chalkboard on the counter told us today's specialty was a Toll House cookie pie.

"Hetty, tell us what Miss Lucy said about this one." I smiled at her as I took out my debit card.

"Well, you know Miss Lucy," Hetty said. "She thinks the pies speak for themselves. She doesn't get into all that stuff about selling you something. You either want it or you don't. That's how Miss Lucy is."

Barb answered immediately, "Oh, we want it, no worries about that."

"I figured as much," Hetty said as she boxed and tied up the pies. "To be sure, she did say one thing. This pie is like a giant chocolate chip cookie wrapped in a pie crust. Can you imagine anything more delicious? I wish we could talk her into doing pies more than once a week, but I think that may be a lost cause. Maybe someday."

As we wedged our pie boxes between us in Barb's cart, I realized that I was now aboard for Barb's whole ride that day. The simple fact that I could welcome such a sudden change in plans pleasantly surprised me. Spontaneity like this would have been unthinkable just a few months ago—yet, there I was, content and looking forward to whatever small pleasures lay ahead of us. Barb drove down Old Port Passage Way toward the community farm as we talked about her next stops.

"What's going on at Allen's?" she asked me suddenly as she jerked the wheel and turned into the T-Shirt Gallery's parking area—a mix of dirt and the island's distinctive tabby, a building material made partly of crushed oyster shells.

"It looks like you are abandoning us!" Barb shouted to Allen as we both climbed out of the cart. Allen was standing on the wide front porch of his store, surrounded by boxes and he several overflowing trash bins at the base of the front steps. The bed of a pickup truck parked diagonally across the lot was also filled with boxes. The scene reminded me of my many moves from house to house.

"The time has come, Barb! Going to move closer to my grandkids," he said and sighed. "The business has just fizzled. Christmas sales never materialized this year. Last year was bad, too. Just can't do it anymore. I sit here and sell a shirt or two, but the stuff is just not moving."

"I didn't know it was that bad," she said.

"Oh, come on now. You must have known, Barb—" and he paused as if searching for words while he taped up the tops of several boxes. He shook his head as he said, "You know I used to love sitting here day after day, talking to the visitors, catching up with our folks. It's very quiet now, too quiet. I can't do it. I don't want to."

He seemed resigned to the move. He wiped his glasses on his shirt, put them back on, and stared at Barb. For such a tall man, his slumped shoulders made him seem burdened, smaller than I remember him when we first set foot in his store with our kids.

"You're really leaving, Allen? How many years has it been?" Barb asked. "You've been here longer than Boyd—and his pottery has been here forever!"

"A long time!" he said. "But this shouldn't be too much of a surprise. You both can do the numbers in your head. Who can make a living selling a couple of shirts a week?" The air was heavy with our mutual disappointment. For this small island, with only a few hundred year-round residents, losses of all kinds reverberated through the community. Finally, he sat down on one of his taped-up boxes.

"Grab a seat," he said to us. That morning, both of us were living on Barb's clock, which seemed to have all the time in the world. So, Barb and I stepped up and each took a seat on a box. For a while we went back and forth about the island's changes, including the pressure the resort's gift shop put on other small businesses.

Allen mainly wanted us to listen. "Believe me, it's taken me a while to get to this point," he said. "How do you leave someplace like this? For a long time, I couldn't imagine living anywhere else, but you can only ignore what you sweep under the rug for so long. Time to face the music, so to speak. Shirts aren't always the souvenirs the tourists want these days. Used to be that everyone bought one, and maybe a sweatshirt, too. But now people want higher end gifts—or many just use their own pictures as souvenirs. It seems the only way to survive would be to find something else that people want while they're on the island. Or maybe a place for people to sit down and spend some time together. Maybe if I'd been running a little restaurant or coffee shop or ice cream parlor, but—I guess, that's all history now. Maybe if I had seen it all sooner, maybe then … ." He didn't finish the what-ifs and the could-haves.

My mind started drifting, as it had more often since arriving on the island. It was right there, while sitting on those cardboard boxes along Allen's porch, that Books & Brew was born.

Just like that—I had my new purpose. It had long been a someday idea of having my own business focused on something I loved—reading. One of my favorite things to do was to find an author I enjoyed and eagerly anticipate his or her next book. Cracking open the cover of a new edition gave me a joy I always imagined sharing with others, but that idea had always seemed like a dream. Today, I unexpectedly was given this gift of opportunity. It was the very first time in a long time that I saw a real future life for me.

I could picture the boxes where we were settled becoming rockers—perhaps similar to the rockers that lined the Inn's front porch for its guests. Or maybe, I would splurge on new teak Kingsley Bate rocking chairs. They caught my eye at a store on the mainland and they would be perfect for this store and my vision. Those rockers were solid and uncomplicated—exactly what made them so inviting for this porch. The tall backs of Charleston-style rockers provided strength and structure, but their curved seat and wide arms would easily fit a computer, a cup of tea, or glass of lemonade while allowing someone the comfort to spread out.

There was no other bookstore on the island and I could see that Allen was right: our island needed more places to gather—for visitors and year-round residents as well. I saw a clear opportunity for my vision for Books & Brew. We agreed to lease terms, an occupancy date, and we shook hands to seal our agreement. Allen would send along the paperwork. I would need to get busy with a business plan.

Allen and I both recognized my new store was both a beginning and an end, as life is. I was grateful to Allen for helping me nurture a seed that had been planted long ago. That whole week, I found myself back in my comfortable professional role of long days of research, developing my plan, contacting suppliers, and putting my own touches on Allen's shop.

I was opening a bookstore!

Chapter 4

The next month was a blur of finalizing my plan, setting up the business, and purchasing, receiving, and displaying the inventory. I knew I had to start small, which fit the cozy size of the store. The oak shelves Allen left behind were perfect for books. One wall lined with tall shelves anchored the room. The opposing wall had shorter shelves that I filled with recently released books or authors I wanted to feature. I moved a few overstuffed club chairs from the Atlanta house into the center of this room, along with a rug that used to be in Meredith's room. The dark indigo color was perfect for this setting and the room's natural light brightened it without being harsh. The rug did not cover all the reclaimed wood floors, and I was happy about that.

I loved the small kitchenette in the back, where I could brew the hot and iced tea that was a defining feature of my new shop. The dining manager at the Inn connected me to his beverage distributor. It was through that connection I met a specialty tea vendor who supplied me with my first inventory. The worn wooden counter at the back of the store would hold the cash register. I found the perfect, old-fashioned model at an open-air antique market in Savannah. Along the counter, there also was plenty of room for my carafes of tea.

In addition to the farm table and chairs, the back room also had a few shelves that would be perfect for book trades. In two corners of the room that everyone had started to call the Trading Floor, I put oversized pillows I had toted along to Mongin from Nicholas's and Meredith's bedrooms. Maybe someone would curl up there during their visit.

On another whim, I added a bell above the main door that would twinkle every time it opened. The sound made me smile with nostalgia, thinking of an identical bell from my own childhood outside my favorite penny candy store on Cape Cod. I was surprised by how little I had to alter from Allen's years in the shop. One favorite feature I inherited was the metal roof over the store and its front porch. The rhythmic sound of rain on the roof automatically made me want to curl up and pull a favorite volume from a nearby shelf. This was the kind of store I wanted—a comfortable place that was inviting and built memories people would smile about for years.

To personalize Books & Brew with my own island story, I pulled out the fifteen-year-old issue of *South Carolina Shores* from my keepsake box. I had the pages professionally matted and set in a bleached wood frame I could hang above the shelves along one wall.

The bell rang.

"Carr, this is amazing! You've done so much! You're about ready! When do y'all officially open?" I recognized Helen's voice, heavy with a creamy southern accent, from the doorway. "It's just the perfect blend of old and new!"

I did not feel ready.

"Helen, you truly are this island's cheerleader! Look around, I still have a way to go." I laughed nervously. I knew I had made progress, but that did not change the fact I had a lot to learn about running my own bookstore.

Helen was now standing in the room with me and smiled. She took my hands, "You *are* amazing. You came here and made yourself part of our fabric. You know as well as I do that we could just continue ordering our books online. But you are making this part of the community and making sure everyone can be a part of it. This is a blessing for us. You are a blessing!" She looked deeply into my eyes and her sincerity bolstered me, the melody of her voice gave me some confidence. I wanted this to work for the island and for me.

"By the way, I am already planning to host our book club here, does that work for you? We won't take up too much room, but there are four of us who are die-hards and maybe two or three others who join on and off depending on the season. How about we use this table in here?" she asked over her shoulder as she studied the back room. Her small, sun-freckled hands were wrapped around the tall chair back and her copper-colored hair shone under the dark bronze forged-iron chandelier hanging above the table.

"How can I refuse you?" I asked, and we both laughed. I already had regular customers and the store wasn't even going to open officially for a few more weeks.

I heard tires crunch and soon enough the bell rang again. That was definitely a sound I could get used to, I thought to myself, smiling.

"Hey Carr, good to see you again," Carl said over the top of an armload of boxes. "Brought a few boxes. Should I put them in the back room?"

"Carl, thank you. Yes, the back room will be great. Tripp has been sorting through some donations and I know he will love to dig into your boxes. And—who is this little guy?" I bent down to get a better look of Carl's sweet companion, a young black pup with a white fluffy chest and brushes of white on three of his paws.

Carl called over his shoulder, "That's Buddy. Don't worry, he loves people." I could see that was true. Buddy was lying on his side with his paw in the air, allowing me to give him a thorough belly rub.

In a minute, Carl was back in the main room and walked over to the wall where my *Shores* article was hanging. I wanted to be able to see it from multiple vantage points so I put it near the center of the store as a reminder to me that it all started from this. "This is the article that you read—that started your Mongin Island journey?" Carl asked and he looked at me, grinning.

"Yes! The very one. I had it framed on the mainland and thought it would be something others would enjoy, too. Have you seen it before?" I replied.

"I have actually, Carr. And, I have to come clean. I am one of the people who was interviewed for this story. I am 'Coastal Carl'—the real estate broker they mentioned, along with some of the other long-time islanders," he laughed as he looked at my astonished face. "You look like I could knock you over with a feather!"

"This is both a strange and wonderful coincidence. You're a celebrity, I guess." I smiled at him. "I had never really put those pieces together. I read that story for all the information about the resort, including the Inn and the amenities, and all the nature, and the island as a whole. I guess the real estate piece never sunk in."

We spoke for a few more minutes about the circumstances of this particular magazine story—and how this piece was a big boost for his sales, which he needed after the real estate market had crashed in 2007.

Buddy had come to stand with us and I bent down to pet him again. I noticed Carl was now quiet and he shifted in place as I looked up at him. "What is it, Carl? You look like something is on your mind. Can I help with something?"

"You can, actually. And, I know, you might say no and that's okay. But I thought I would start with you. It's a big ask and I know that, but—" he replied.

"Carl, for heaven's sake, what is it? It can't be all that bad, can it?" I prompted him.

"Look, I adopted Buddy about three months ago. Now, he is a little under a year old. He is a black Lab mixed with who knows what. The vet thinks he is likely fully grown. I am going to be spending some more time on the mainland and maybe doing some traveling. There are some deals I am exploring, some people I want to meet. These people, well—I guess the thing of it is, with some of these people, I have to be flexible with their schedule. Would you mind if Buddy kept you company? Maybe he could stay with you while I travel and get through this deal. Is this too much—too big of an ask? He really is a good boy, he is trained and all. Doesn't have much to say, really, just a good boy who wants to be with people."

"Carl, honestly, I hadn't thought about getting a dog yet, I just—" I broke off, surprised about how emotional this topic was for me. It was still hard to talk about even though it had been a few years since my own sweet dogs had passed. I felt tears stinging my eyes. I still missed them every day, those lovable, goofy girls who took such good care of our family in their own ways.

He said immediately, "You're right, it is too much, apologies. I guess I just got carried away with what you told me before about your dogs. You know—how you used to bring your two 'girls' here with you and how much they loved the beach, how important they were to your family. I knew you were a dog lover, like me. Buddy here has already been abandoned by his previous owner; I just want him someplace where I know he will be happy. If I knew this project was coming, I may have waited to get a dog, but then I would have missed knowing Buddy."

And that's how I adopted Buddy. I found myself assuring Carl: "Of course Buddy can stay with me and I will take excellent care of him. I can't imagine him thinking he was abandoned again. No dog should know that heartbreak. I can tell he is a sweet baby. But honestly, even if he wasn't, I would still take him. Don't give it another thought, yes. I would be happy to."

Turning to Buddy, I gently stroked his little square head. "We are going to be great pals, right Buddy?"

Buddy gave me a gentle kiss on my cheek.

Chapter 5

The days clicked by and, ready or not, Books & Brew opened. My goal was to welcome customers before the busy tourism season kicked off. My soft opening consisted of a gathering of a few friends two days before the doors officially opened. We sold a few books, drank a lot of tea, and spent a few hours getting more comfortable in the store. There wasn't much to practice, since sales and stocking would move at island pace. The key to the store's success was going to be how people felt being here. Tripp, a retired schoolteacher, was an indispensable hire. He was endlessly available, an avid reader, personable, and happy to be with people. He was the perfect addition.

The day after the soft opening, Tripp and I were putting out new stock, arranging a lot of the books with their covers out to make the shelves look fuller than they were. As sparse as our new stock was, at that point, I was not worried at all. Inventory was still arriving daily, which encouraged customers to keep visiting to check out the new additions. It was an accidentally genius business strategy.

Carl's first few boxes of donations had been an amazing boost to the Trading Floor. The first few swaps happened at the soft opening. Clearly, that room was going to be a hit. Tripp and I planned another visit to Carl's to get more books. If we each drove a cart, we would quickly have some full shelves in this room.

"Tripp, I feel like something is missing in here, what do you think?" I asked him, knowing he would give me a direct answer.

"Well, Carr, you've done a good job with changing things up. You know that I think you absolutely hit it out of the park and the ghosts of the T-Shirt Gallery have been sent packing."

"But?" I probed.

"If you ask me, I think you need something on the walls and more stuff on the tables, more stuff around. The books and chairs and all the things you added since Allen left have made it feel like someone's home, which is great. People love our different rooms. They love the tea, and you were smart to get the resort to include your flyers in each guest room. But there is no—what would you call it? There is no—life. There is no *island* life in here. I think that's it. Once you walk through the front door, honestly, I think it looks like you could be in a bookstore anywhere."

I completely disagreed and pointed to my framed issue of *Shores*.

"That's a start, but it's not quite what I meant," he said.

The last thing I wanted was to fill these rooms with commercial beach décor. Shells, fake starfish, anchors, and nautical-themed knick-knacks were the opposite of what I was trying to do. However, I had asked this question and Tripp had answered. He looked at me expectantly and I knew I had to say something.

"What about some big photographs of places on the island that tell people why we love it here so much? What about some sunset shots over the water or some pictures on the dirt roads, you know, things like that?" I was offering something I could do myself and would be comfortable with displaying in the store.

"Fantastic!" Tripp agreed, although I was still not really sure this was what he had in mind. It wasn't lost on me that he had chosen to be supportive rather than push his viewpoint. I was immediately filled with gratitude to be surrounded by people who were helping me find my way.

I asked him, "Can you watch the store? I am going to run home and grab my camera. I will take some shots and then you can pick the ones you like," offering Tripp the same grace he showed me.

I spent a few hours over the next several days finding the perfect shots. My Nikon D3300 camera was a useful tool. It was an older style digital SLR but with its fast shutter speed, I was able to memorialize some of the everyday Mongin Island magic. I captured deer and fox squirrels and long shots down the dirt roads. I photographed some of the historic sites, including the old ruins of what once had been the tabby walls of homes set back into the woods. I had a wide range of scenes, places, and a mix of colorscapes. But I wanted a really standout sunset shot that would showcase Mongin Island. Watching the sunset and the sunrise were rites of passage here. Could you say you had experienced Mongin Island if you hadn't been soothed by the sun gradually falling below the horizon as the waves rhythmically filed away the sharp edges of anxiety, stress, and disappointment?

Just before closing, I heard the crunch of golf cart tires turning from the road into the store's parking lot. "Barb must need something to read for her beach time tomorrow after she gets her new arrivals settled," Tripp said as he looked out the front window. "Did you notice how Barb always shops in the new books section? I never see her grab a trade."

I smiled at him and replied, "I noticed, yes. Just like you, she finds a way to help without ever saying a word."

"Hey, you!" I greeted her from the porch. "Guess what? The Kingsley Bate rockers I ordered are coming on the barge tomorrow. Tripp got these old ceiling fans working, too. The front porch will be ready in the next day or so. Want to break it in with me?"

"I get first dibs on picking my chair! I want the one with the best view." She grinned as she said it but we both knew she was at least a little serious. She would not want to miss any of the comings and goings on Old Port Passage Way.

"Anything for you! Speaking of views, let me ask you something. I need a sunset or sunrise view over the water. I want to frame something for the back room. We don't get much light in there and I want something that pops for the one wall that faces the doorway. I was thinking about going to the ferry landing. I was thinking if I stood at the beginning of the dock, I could get the tall reeds, the dock, and some boats with the sun in the background. But, I don't know, it just seems so—so basic, you know? I mean for us, we've been there a million times and for new visitors, it just doesn't feel like it tells our story. Any other suggestions?"

"You want something the average visitor probably hasn't experienced?"

I nodded my head.

"Then, we need to go to Governor's Point. I'm not sure about going for a sunset shot. It gets pretty dark back there without any streetlights." She looked at her phone and looked back at me. "Looks like sunrise will be around 6:55 tomorrow morning, which is supposed to be a sunny day. How about I pick you up around 6:30 and we head over? You can see if that's what you're looking for—but I am betting it will be."

Chapter 6

I made us two travel mugs of hot, steamy black coffee and was waiting for Barb on my porch about twelve hours later. We took off immediately.

"This is one of my favorite times of the day," Barb said, clicking on the cart's headlights.

"Every time is your favorite time of the day!" I laughed.

"Not exactly. I don't love property check out and flipping time. All these two- and three-night turnovers are wearing me out. I guess it is a nice problem to have, but it's exhausting! But, you're right. I do love every good day on Mongin Island."

With that, we were off the paved road, heading down the twists and turns of the dirt paths loosely defined as roads. The golf cart bumped over holes and rough patches, making drinking our coffees impossible. The cart groaned and squeaked as we went deeper off-road, running over roots that grew under the paths. There were no street signs, no landmarks. I was relieved I had not tried to find this on my own. Barb expertly maneuvered her way.

"What is this place, Barb? What is Governor's Point?" I realized I had heard of it, but in all my visits, we had never explored it. "It's what, a mile from the ferry? But it feels like we are in the middle of nowhere, a thousand miles from anywhere!"

"It was supposed to be an up-and-coming development. Must be about ten lots or so, with a pool and a little clubhouse. You know, one of those exclusive, small 'waterfront' neighborhoods. They built the pool and sold some of the lots years ago and then everything stopped. There are lots of guesses about what happened—but I don't know that anyone actually has the whole story. No houses were ever built. The pool and the clubhouse are all that's there. A lot of the site is overgrown. You can't even see property lines anymore. Nature has taken over. But there is a dock that takes you right down to an incredible marsh view and you can see the Mongin River. We are on the other side of the island now, away from the beach and ocean. You're right though, we still are only a mile away from the ferry landing, even less from Books & Brew. I like to sit out there on that dock to get away from the crowds sometimes. It's like my own secret hideaway."

She finished as we parked in a spot right in front of the pool.

Her description was perfect. This place was like an afterthought, an idea in which people had lost interest. Development had stalled, like the required effort was just too much work, leaving a sad, neglected plot of land with a sun-bleached sign announcing: "Welcome to Governor's Point" with a phone number for real estate inquiries.

"So, does the developer still own most of these lots?" I asked Barb.

"I assume so, yes, but I'm not really sure. Like I said, I think a few were sold but which ones and who bought them, well, I don't know. I know Coastal Carl was the agent years ago but I didn't really keep up with it all," she said as we finally took our first good sip of coffee and I got my camera ready.

"Coastal Carl," I said. "Now that I met Carl, it's hard for me to think of him being called that. Seems so kitschy, so unlike him."

She laughed, "I agree. It's just one of those ideas that seems like a good one when you're younger I guess and well, some things just stick. Seeing him day in and day out, having so many people call him that so many times, I can't imagine *not* calling him that. He has done very well selling properties that are not part of the resort. Many people have been on at least one side of a deal with Coastal Carl!"

I shook my head, "Will I ever know all these mysteries of Mongin Island?"

"Honestly, probably not. We are an interesting bunch!" Barb said. "Let's get your shot." She showed me the way to the marsh dock. What an amazing site it was!

You could see sparkling water in every direction from the edge of the dock. It was so peaceful, sitting with our legs over the side, listening to the faraway calls of the birds and the constant lapping of the water on the dock pylons. The sky started to turn pink. It looked like someone had painted the sky with a pastel brush. It was breathtaking and another of these mysterious, hidden spots on Mongin Island that made you feel like it belonged just to you.

"I can see why this is your special spot," I whispered, trying hard not to ruin this moment. "People would kill for a view like this." I quickly took a bunch of shots. Tripp was going to have a tough time picking just one for the Trading Floor. It didn't seem like you could get a bad picture here—about as close to perfection as you could imagine.

Barb nodded. "I never get tired of this view. I hope these lots are never developed. If they were, I'm not sure a homeowner would appreciate us strolling around back here." She smiled, but her eyes were sad.

"It looks pretty forgotten, maybe we will stay lucky," I said, trying to lighten the mood. "Unfortunately, I have to get back to the store. Tripp is picking up the rockers from the barge and I want to be at the store to help him unload. Would love to come back here with you—that's for sure."

We gathered our cups, put our shoes back on, and started down the dock. Barb's flip-flops snapped in a quick tempo.

"What a great way to start the day, thanks Barb," I said as we got to the cart. "It really is a shame, this property could be out of this world, especially given the small size of this neighborhood." I looked over at the pool and noticed an unlatched gate in the protective fence surrounding it. "Hold on Barb, let me latch this. I would hate for something to happen if any of the kids got back here. I will feel better if it is at least somewhat secure, not that this gate actually does much—but—" I said over my shoulder.

The pool did not look inviting at all. Filled with still green water, algae, and overgrown plants, it was hard to even imagine this being what was advertised on the sign posted only a few feet away. The pool deck bubbled in places where tree roots were pushing up from beneath the ground. I pulled the rusty gate forward to the post and something caught my eye. Was that a shoe on the cement, near the pool steps? I looked again and saw something dark beneath the water's surface. Looking back at Barb, I called: "Just a minute, Barb! Something is in here!"

"What? What did you say?" When I didn't answer, she came to the fence.

"Barb!" I yelled, "Barb, come quick, I think someone is in here. I think someone is at the bottom of the pool!" I was screaming as my eyes focused. With my heart pounding in my ears, I could not hear her response. "Call the police!" we yelled to each other at the same time, but she beat me to actually doing it. She dialed as I stood looking from her to the pool. I was frantically searching for something I could use to reach this person—some kind of pool equipment, a pole, a large branch, anything. We were in the middle of nowhere with a body in this abandoned pool.

"Dispatcher said they will come soon." Barb tried to sound reassuring. Before I could answer, I heard her talking to someone else, giving me a concerned look. She shook her head from side to side. She spoke into her phone: "Yes, in the pool. At the bottom of the pool." She paused, then seemed to be answering a question. "I don't know, I mean, maybe. Okay, we won't."

As she hung up, she told me she called the island firehouse directly to speed up the response because the central emergency dispatcher is on the mainland. "At the firehouse, Sarabeth told me she'll get someone out here, soon, Carr. But she made it clear that we should step back. She said, 'Do not go into that water.' Sarabeth said there were all kinds of things dumped in there over the years. I guess people tried to manage the pool on their own for a while, then abandoned it. No one knows what's in there."

I understood. I was glued to this spot.

Mongin Island has no full-time police force, so the first responders were the firemen who came through the woods in both the ladder truck and their Suburban. In a matter of minutes, Governor's Point was bursting with activity. Because the fire staff are also paramedics, they rolled in with stretchers, crash kits, and bags filled with devices, equipment, and medicine. Another team, in dive suits, was quickly in the water, hoping this was a rescue.

All too soon, it was obvious this was a recovery.

"Hold up! Hold up!" Chief Lancaster's booming voice stopped everyone in their tracks. "Someone from the sheriff's department will be here soon. Let's not touch anything else."

"Charlie!" he yelled to the young cadet standing near the truck, "You're in charge of keeping everyone else out of this area. Grab some cones and block the road up there." He nodded in the general direction of the path we had traveled. Charlie scuttled off, looking relieved to be doing something.

Chief Lancaster called to us: "Ladies, please wait by your golf cart for the sheriff's department. They will be here soon. They will want to talk to you, I'm sure of it."

"Aren't they coming all the way from the mainland?" I asked Barb.

Andrew, who had been on the ladder truck and overheard me, explained that an officer usually came to Mongin Island on Tuesdays, Thursdays, and Saturdays. Someone already had been en route when our call came in, so they should be on the island and at Governor's Point any minute.

"What usually happens in cases like this?" I whispered to Barb. I wanted her to tell me what to do, what to expect. I wanted someone to be in control and I wanted that someone to not be me.

"Cases like this? What are you talking about? We don't have cases like this! Someone is dead, Carr. I mean, it's not like he just fell into the pool on his afternoon stroll. Who knows how long he has been

in there? I mean—this doesn't happen here. This can't be happening!"
Barb's voice had risen until she was shouting. Her hands were shaking and her eyes were wide.

"I'm sorry," we said at the same time. I hugged her.

"I'm going to take some pictures," I decided. "I'm going to take
some shots of the ground, the shrubs around the pool, I don't know,
I am just going to see what might be helpful. I have to do something."
I walked away and started taking a few pictures, not really knowing
what I was looking for. Barb was staring at the chaotic scene in play
in front of us. Even the professionals did not know exactly what to
do next, but I was careful to stay out of their way. We were all in
uncharted territory.

When a sheriff's Jeep came rolling along the dirt road, I was
flooded with relief. There was a part of me that felt somehow an officer would pop out of the car with all the answers. They would glance
around, tell us what unfortunate accident had befallen whoever was
in the pool and everything would make sense. We would be able to go
back to our easy-going, peaceful life, with the only challenge facing us
being the upcoming influx of seasonal visitors and travelers. I wanted
all that to happen, even though it was hardly realistic.

So, when Deputy Julie climbed out of the Jeep, Chief Lancaster
was immediately at her side.

"Deputy," the Chief greeted her. "Ma'am, we have a situation you
need to see," he said as they walked quickly to the pool. There was no
time for small talk. The air seemed to be getting heavier with humidity and the reality of what had likely unfolded here.

We waited for Deputy Julie to approach us.

"Ladies, thank you for your patience and for calling us for help,"
Deputy Julie said. "I am here to help. We are going to figure out what
happened. So, to help you, I need you to help me, okay?" Julie's tight
curls spilled way past her shoulders.

"Of course, yes. What can we do?" I asked. "I mean we didn't really
see anything. We were just walking to our cart." Julie's eyes, heavily
lined in teal, and her bright lipstick, were riveting to me. Her makeup

was so distracting it forced me to block out everything else that was happening to focus solely on Julie.

"Tell me about it," she encouraged. "Tell me everything you remember."

Barb and I began with our arrival here to take some photos—and ended with seeing the shadow in the pool. Deputy Julie listened to our story and wrote a few notes in her book as we spoke, looking up at us as she encouraged us to continue. I told her about the pictures I took while the first responders were examining the scene. I offered to send them to her, which she appreciated. She handed us her card and sent us on our way, reminding us to call her if we remembered any other details.

"I have to know," I called out to her, "Deputy, I have to know before I go. Had this person already passed? I mean, there wasn't anything we could have or should have done? I feel like I should have done more than just stand here and wait. Should I have jumped into that water? I just, I just wasn't—I don't know—I guess prepared? I just wasn't prepared for this—I don't know what I am trying to say—I guess, was there anything I could have done to help this person?" My words were tumbling out faster than I intended.

"No, absolutely not. You both did all the right things. People handle situations like this in all different ways and not always in ways you see on television, being some hero. Your reaction was what most people do as they try to make sense of what they are seeing. In this case, it is best you didn't enter that water unprotected. Unfortunately, our victim has likely been in there for at least a day, maybe more. We will know more soon. Go home, get some rest and let us know if something, anything, else comes to you." With that, she was off in the direction of the rescue crew, her hair extending like a small cape behind her.

We walked like zombies to our cart and somehow climbed in. Everything was happening in some kind of altered state. Before we knew it, we headed back down the dirt road in stunned silence. Although we didn't know it yet, we were part of a Mongin Island murder.

Chapter 7

"There you are! I called you a ton of times. The barge was late so I came to the store first to wait. It got in over an hour ago. Merle said the rockers were there at the barge landing. Didn't want to leave the store but I will head down now that you're back ... What's wrong? What happened?" Tripp said all at once, his excitement quickly turning to curiosity and then to concern. "Why are you just sitting there? Come on, get out and come here. What happened?" His long legs brought him to the cart instantly. "Come on, girls, I've got you."

"My God, Tripp. It was awful," Barb said. As we started to explain everything, he walked with us to the front porch, up the stairs, and then got us settled in the club chairs in the middle of the large room. Tripp's presence was so soothing, his voice so reassuring, we felt immediately comforted by him. The store was almost empty except for one customer near the nonfiction shelves. Once we saw him, we immediately stopped talking. Tripp and Barb exchanged a look that I could not decipher. I looked at them questioningly but neither offered any comment. Tripp got busy making tea and I stood up to greet the customer.

"Hello, welcome to Books & Brew. Can I help you find anything?" I was hoping the smile I plastered on my face looked remotely authentic as I took a few steps closer to the tall shelves.

"Wonderful addition, lovely store indeed." This stranger with a polished British accent smiled at me and extended his hand. "I'm Paul Easton. It's a pleasure to meet you." I took a long look at him and saw he was well dressed, his tailored clothes were well made and were not the usual casual, laid-back island attire most people sported. There was a formality to him, a rigidness in his perfectly polite demeanor.

"Paul, hello," I said. "I am Carr, glad you stopped in. We've only been open for a few weeks. We are still getting in inventory, adding our own touches, and actually working on planning some social events here at the store. Are you here for a visit?"

"Carr, *hmm*, interesting name. What is the derivation?"

"Carissa. So, Paul, are you staying locally—or are you just here for the day?" My head was full of the scene we just left at the pool, all the unanswered questions, and my nerves were frayed. I was not in the mood for verbal Ping Pong.

"A woman of grace, as I recall its meaning. Beautiful name, certainly." Again, he didn't answer. "It appears I have arrived at an inopportune time. I will leave you to it." He looked briefly at the three of us and settled his gaze on me. "Perhaps tomorrow will suit you better, as I do have some inquiries regarding your nonfiction section. I shall return then." He dismissed us and saw himself out the door.

"He looks so familiar," Barb blurted out before the door was even shut. The bell above it was still slightly ringing. "Isn't that the guy who rents the old Baxter house, near the school?"

"That's it!" Tripp said, slapping his hand on the counter. "I've been trying to place him myself since he walked in. I think I remember seeing him at the coffee shop in the mornings last year. He insisted they buy a ceramic teapot to serve his tea. I remember how Brian rolled his eyes behind the counter."

"Yes! That's who it is! He was a long-term renter who always wanted a place close to the ferry, away from the resort. Didn't he stay for a few weeks or a month or so? I remember seeing him and talking to him a few times."

"Very opinionated," Tripp said.

"That's him," she said.

They certainly weren't selling me on him. He sounded like exactly the kind of person I would usually go out of my way to avoid.

"Coastal Carl would know," Tripp said. "Baxter uses him for his rentals. He rents out his house by the school and he also has a villa on Beach Road. I think Carl handles both properties."

"Coastal Carl—his ears must be ringing," I smiled. "This is the second time today we are talking about him!"

I asked Tripp to lock the front door and turn our sign to 'Closed'. The idea of serving customers and making small talk was just too much. "And Tripp, please go get those rockers. I know Merle will want them off the barge loading area. Do you mind?"

"Are you sure you two will be alright?" He looked from Barb to me and then back again. "I will probably be about an hour, round trip, by the time I load up and all."

Barb answered immediately, "We will be okay, go ahead. The sooner you get back, the sooner we can be done and out of here."

"You go too, Barb. Tripp, when you get back, can you drop me by my house?"

"You got it, boss," he said over his shoulder as he headed toward his truck. "Be back as soon as I can."

Barb was hesitant. "You sure you are okay if I leave you here? I have a couple of checkouts and I, honestly, I don't know ..." Her voice trailed off. We all were feeling the stress of the day.

I said nothing—I knew her well enough by now to just wait her out.

Before she followed Tripp out the door, Barb took a big breath. "I just can't believe this happened today. I mean, I know people die—people do die on this island. I know. It's just that they usually are older or sick and they die in their houses or the clinic—and, well, I guess there was that one person who had a heart attack on the beach. But I have lived here for about twenty-five years—and no one dies in a deserted pool in the middle of the woods. It feels like something really bad happened to whoever that was. I feel sick." She looked sick, too, her face was white, her lips were tight and the crease between her brows was very pronounced.

"Look Barb, let's wait to see what we learn from the deputy. It could be a very, very unfortunate accident. We don't know. Maybe it just feels creepy because of the way Governor's Point looks, the pool, and all the overgrown stuff. You go ahead, I will call you later. Are *you* sure you're okay?"

"I am okay, I guess," she said softly as she unlocked the door and headed to her cart. I watched her drive away, made myself a fresh cup of tea, and sat in one of the club chairs. I kicked off my shoes and curled my legs up on the cushion. As I closed my eyes, I replayed the scene over and over. I thought about Barb, too. I know she is a strong, resilient woman, but as much as I love Mongin Island, she loves it that much more. She has lived many seasons of her life here. We were going to have to get each other through this—although I knew Barb would bristle if I was obvious in trying to help her. She would be the first to help someone else, but that someone else needed to be anyone else but herself.

Those thoughts must have taken me miles away because I was jolted back to the store by the insistent knock on the door. I sat another minute, hoping whoever was demanding entry would see the Closed sign and be on their way. No such luck, and now the knocking sounded closer to pounding.

"Hello, Carr! Are you here?" I heard Deputy Julie's voice as she simultaneously rang my phone.

I walked to the door and opened it for her.

"Hey, sorry, can I come in?" she asked as she put her phone into her pocket. Three quick strides of her long legs and she was in the middle of the room.

"Certainly, has something else happened? What's going on?" I felt my nerves tingle. Her presence alone put me on full alert.

"I am sorry to tell you that the gentleman in the pool has been tentatively identified. The coroner will be doing an autopsy later today and we should have more direction first thing in the morning. It is my understanding this person lived alone, here on the island, but we are trying to find out a little more that may help positively identify him. Would you be willing to help?"

"Of course, but I am not sure what else I can tell you."

"We found a wallet in his pocket. We think this is Carl Tibbons. Do you know him?"

"Carl Tibbons?" I looked at her in disbelief. "No, please, that can't be true."

"It appears to be true," Julie said, then explained that a positive identification was tricker than it might seem in this case. "So, Carr, you do know this man?" Julie was gently trying to get me to focus, but that now familiar feeling of grief was creeping its ugly, hateful fingers back around my heart.

I don't know how long I sat there, trying to make sense of what Julie was saying and of the idea that this wonderful, generous man, clearly loved by so many here, was dead. Finally, I said, "If it is Carl, then yes. I met him when I was setting up the shop. He had been so welcoming and kind, everyone loved him. All I hear is how many people live here on this island because of him. He loved this island, these people."

Julie spoke slowly and carefully, "So, that is who was selling the Governor's Point real estate? That's whose name was on that sign? Okay, this is good information."

"I am stunned, honestly," I admitted. "Completely stunned. I don't know what else to say."

"You know, I am not here all day, every day," she said. "Depending on what happens with the coroner's report, I likely will be here more often but still—since you're here full-time and the locals will soon find out you were the person who found Mr. Tibbons, you may hear things that I won't. Would you mind keeping your eyes and ears open? Would you mind if we stay in contact? I've lived in this county long enough to know how the local code works."

"Of course, I will do what I can. If someone did this to him, if this is not some weird accident, if Carl was intentionally injured, you can be sure I will help you find the—the *low-life* who did this. I can assure you, I won't be the only one who will want to help find the person who hurt Carl."

Julie looked at me directly and replied, "I have a feeling you are used to being in charge, making decisions, and getting people to do things. I think people will tell you what they know or, at least, their theories. They will want to bounce their ideas off you because you were there. It would be really helpful to hear this stuff. People sometimes know more than they think."

I nodded.

"I appreciate it, and I am sorry for the loss of your neighbor," she said gently as she walked to the door. "I will call you tomorrow. Thanks again." With that, she was gone and the room was once again quiet, but not empty. It was filled with her lingering presence and the weight of what she implied. Although she didn't say it directly, it felt like Barb could be right: This didn't feel like an accident.

In short order, Tripp returned to the store, the rockers were unloaded and placed on the porch. It was hardly the celebration we thought it would be. We agreed we were done for the day so we shut everything down and locked up. I called for Buddy and jumped into Tripp's cart. A few minutes later, Tripp dropped us back at my house. Closing my door, I inhaled deeply and was glad for the quiet of my own home. I took a long shower, made lunch, and poured myself some spearmint iced tea. I brought my plate of berries, yogurt, and granola and my glass to the coffee table in the family room and flopped down on my overstuffed sofa. I was physically and emotionally drained.

I texted Barb: "Hey, I know you are busy. You okay?"

"All good, I guess. Any news?" she texted back after a few minutes.

"Julie found Carl Tibbons' wallet on the body. We will know more, prob tomorrow."

My phone rang immediately, "The guy in the pool is Coastal Carl? Are you kidding me? Is she sure?" Barb asked all at once. She had gone right from the store to her own work with her rental properties and I could hear in her voice that she was reaching the end of her rope.

"Julie is reasonably sure it's Carl, but only because his wallet with his ID was in the pocket of the victim, and of course, the physical description seems like a match." I paused and considered whether to tell Barb the rest right now. I decided she should know. "Julie did explain that it's difficult to identify a body in a case like this because of whatever chemicals were in the pool. We will know more tomorrow, until then it is just her theory. I can't believe it, Barb. He was just at the store a few days ago. He was going to travel, he had plans. How does this happen?"

Barb was silent for a while. "Something is definitely not right," she said at last. "I mean, I didn't know Carl's daily schedule but I know he never traveled for weeks at a time. I thought it was weird when he asked you to take Buddy. Something is wrong. We need to get to Julie and make a plan. She asked you to help and get involved?"

"She did, why?"

"I could tell by the way she was watching you, talking to you at Governor's Point. Are you sure this is good for you? Are you sure you want to be involved in this? You know how it is on the island, everyone is going to be coming to you with opinions and theories. You know this, right? You're going to be talking about death and loss, are you sure all this is good for you? You were just getting your feet under you. I'm not sure, Carr, I am not sure this is the right thing for you. At least not right now, anyway."

Is it possible to experience peace and anger at the same time? I don't know how else to describe what I was feeling. Barb's care and concern filled me up, but I was angry that someone would hurt one of our own. "I have to, Barb, I have to do it. If I can help, I am going to. It is what Carl would have done. It is what we all do around here. And—I'm fairly certain it is what Rob would have wanted me to do."

"Then count me in too. Let's call Julie and see what's next."

Chapter 8

If Julie had been surprised that Barb and I were a package deal, she didn't say it. She asked if we would stop by Carl's house to see if we could find out more about Carl's travels and what he had been working on. So, although it had already been quite a day, we agreed to head over to the lighthouse as soon as Barb had her visitors settled.

It had been years since I visited the lighthouse and the museum housed in the front room. It was one of those places you went to once, maybe twice, and then you checked it off the list. It looked nothing like a traditional lighthouse. If you didn't know better, you would assume it was someone's house—maybe the lighthouse keeper's home. Its white wooden frame was nestled in the greenery and palm trees that lined the dirt road. If you looked closely, you could see the large dormer where the light was kept. Other than that, there wasn't much to see. The kids were somewhat disappointed it wasn't a light-house with a spiral staircase you could climb for an amazing ocean view. We had been to Huntington Island, South Carolina, several times and climbed dozens and dozens of steps that led to the narrow walkway at the top of the lighthouse there. In size and scale, this one didn't really compare.

Historically, the Mongin Island lighthouse was interesting because it had both a front range and a rear range light. The kids found it unbelievable the government paid less than $500 for the lighthouse land and were amused by the stories of mules pulling carts to move the lighthouse from one place to another as the shoreline shifted through the years. Other than that, the museum did not hold their interest. Without panoramic ocean views and a commanding presence of a tower to climb, it was just another house. No matter how many times we drove by on the way to the beach, there was never really a crowd. Today was no different, even for a Saturday. On the weekends, or "turnover days" as we called them, some of the local attractions usually had an influx of visitors who either arrived before check-in or were waiting for their boat departure. The lighthouse never seemed to benefit from this routine.

It was surrounded by houses with year-round residents. Maybe Carl's neighbors would be able to fill in some details about Carl and what he had been up to the last few days. It was quiet and the air was still as we walked up the wooden steps to the museum. I tugged on the door, which did not open, and waited a few minutes to see if someone had heard me. Our knocks went unanswered, so we took the gravel path to the back door. The crunching stones beneath our feet seemed unnaturally loud—surely someone would hear, I thought. I saw a well-worn pair of boat shoes, brown duck boots, and a ceramic dog bowl at the base of the small steps. After a few minutes of knocking and a few unanswered "Hellos?", I turned the knob and we found ourselves in Carl's small kitchen. The house was stuffy. There were some glasses in the sink and coffee in the pot on the coffee maker. There were a few pieces of mail and a folder, opened on the table. It looked like Carl had just stepped away and would be back any minute—even though I knew that was not likely to be true.

"Can I ask what you think you are doing here?" a female voice broke the silence.

Barb and I both jumped.

"Clearly you can see that this is not the lighthouse, right?" A young woman in jeans, flip flops, and a Mongin T-shirt stood there looking at us.

"I am so sorry, I thought Carl lived alone. I just didn't realize—" I started to answer her.

The woman interrupted, "Sorry, but the museum's closed for a few days. And the lighthouse isn't open to the public."

Of course, I thought. We looked like tourists. I finally extended my hand. "No, we're not tourists. We're Carl's friends. I am Carr and this is Barb." The woman shook my hand but said nothing more.

"I didn't get your name," Barb said, extending her hand.

"I didn't give it. As if Theresa isn't bad enough, now you two?" Her voice was tight and her face was bright red. With one hand on her hip, she waved her dismissal into the air with the other. She was absolutely done with us before we could even start explaining. Without another word, she turned her back and started to leave the house.

"Wait, please, wait!" I called after her. Catching up to her in the side yard, I said, "I think there has been some kind of misunderstanding. I own Books & Brew—down the road? The new bookstore?"

She blinked but showed no recognition. "Do you think I am some kind of a fool? Pretty bad for you to just waltz in here. What are you doing, getting more clothes for Carl?"

We stood facing each other in the side yard as a rising wind blew our hair in our faces and the bright sun made us squint at each other. The last few minutes were a jumble of emotions and I felt dangerously close to either laughing or crying. I wasn't sure if she was going to scream at me, hit me, or just keep walking away. She looked down and said, "I knew I couldn't trust him. I mean, if I knew it would end this way, I would never have said anything." Her voice was a whisper now.

"I think there has been a misunderstanding," I said. "Can we start again?" I smiled gently at her and hoped she would meet my eyes. Receiving nothing but a slight shrug, I took a deep breath. I was not prepared for the possibility of bumping into someone who actually knew Carl this well. "I'm sorry we got off to a bad start. I am Carr

Jepson and I am sorry we have not met before now. What did you say your name was?"

"I didn't say it was anything—" but then she offered: "I am Missy. I am Carl's neighbor and—I'm his friend. I am Carl's friend. I live there." She pointed to the small, blue cottage peeking out from an overgrown shrub to my right.

"Well Missy, I don't know how we haven't bumped into each other before now, but I live on Captain Morgan Lane and Barb also lives on the resort property. It's only a couple of minutes from here." She was largely unmoved by any of this as she looked me up and down.

Barb tried her luck, "Have you lived next to Carl long?"

"Long enough."

"Long enough for what?" Barb asked, clearly running out of patience.

"Long enough to know you two are sticking your nose into something. I've been here for a few months. I keep my boat at the other side of the island, at the county dock. It's why I rented here. I can get in and out without any crowds. I don't take that public ferry, don't eat at the fancy restaurants. Just want some quiet. Carl knows that."

This was only going to get more difficult. "Missy, we were at Governor's Point today and experienced something we were not expecting—involving Carl, I mean. Is there someplace we could sit for a few minutes and talk?"

Her face went from pink to red to flaming. "We can talk right here if it is all the same to you. I don't need you trying to work me over. You have some nerve, coming here and—"

"Okay, Missy, this is making it harder than it already is but here is the truth: Today, when we were at Governor's Point—"

"Why would anyone go there? What were you doing there? Sticking your nose into things that don't concern you?"

"Missy, just walk with me," I directed and surprisingly, she did. We all sat at the picnic table in Carl's yard. From this view, I could see into her backyard and I noticed a large magnolia tree at the edge of Missy's yard. It was a beautiful and peaceful spot.

To answer Missy's question of why we were at Governor's Point, I began with my desire to take pictures and ended with Julie's tentative identification of Carl. We sat in silence and then her tears started and she shook her head as if she was rejecting this information as a fabricated story.

"I knew something was wrong. I knew it wasn't just Theresa," she eventually said. Even knowing her for only these few minutes, I understood Missy would talk only at her own pace and answer only what she wanted to, so I settled myself and gave her the space she needed to continue. Eventually, she narrated her own story that meandered through moving to Mongin Island only a couple of months ago, meeting Carl, and their evolving relationship. They began as neighbors, became friends, dated—and had wound up not speaking. The twice-maligned Theresa was a recent island visitor who lived on the mainland. According to Missy, Carl met her at some real estate conference on the mainland, they exchanged numbers and had started seeing each other in recent weeks.

"I don't know what went wrong with us," Missy said. "I told Carl I was allergic to Buddy. I mean, he is a great dog, but I could not spend any amount of time in his house and Buddy could not come inside mine. I think that's what ended us. Carl was like, 'love me, love my dog' and when I said I wouldn't or actually, I couldn't, well that was it. Carl stopped coming over, stopped texting, he never actually said it was over but I saw Theresa here and some islanders saw Carl with her over on the mainland at the restaurants on the docks. God, so embarrassing! What a fool I have been. And now it just gets lonely here—you know how it is," she looked up at me suddenly. "I mean the guy chose his dog over me. That tells you everything you need to know."

"I do know how it is. It can get lonely here," I said, "but I am sure Carl thought—" I stopped, mad at myself for doing the thing I hated that people did to me after Rob died. I hated the "air bubbles", as I called them, the things people said to fill the air when they didn't know what else to say. Truth be told, I wasn't actually sure of anything—least of all anything that had to do with Carl. Who was I to say what I am sure about? I stopped talking. She was gazing off into the distance, not focused on any one thing that I could see. I kept my eyes on her face, my eyes were ready to meet hers.

"I knew something was wrong when he didn't come home," she said, finally facing me. "So, what else do you know?"

There weren't many details, but we shared everything we had learned from Deputy Julie, Chief Lancaster, and the others who were on the scene at Governor's Point. I refrained from showing Missy the pictures I took. There wasn't much for her to see but I felt the pictures from the pool would be an unnecessary jolt.

"Tell us more about the last few days with Carl," I said. "I know Deputy Julie will be checking in tomorrow or maybe even later today. We want to give her some of this background."

"Do you think someone did this to Carl?" she asked. "I mean, that must have been what happened, right? He didn't just fall into that pool, right?"

Barb answered, "It's too soon to know, Missy. It is just too soon. I know it's hard, but we have to be patient."

She did tell us a little more about the last few days. Carl had been on and off the island a lot recently, sometimes even having the water taxi from the mainland pick him up for last minute meetings. Missy had seen Carl waiting at the county dock a few times while she tended to her own boat. He never asked to borrow hers.

Sometimes—and she couldn't remember exactly when—she found visitors walking around Carl's front lawn. They were surprised that the museum was closed after an unanticipated change in its schedule. On Wednesday, she saw Carl as he was headed out for a walk. He went his usual route, to the beach. Missy remembered Carl casually waving, but he had not stopped even though she was busy in her front yard picking up some small branches and twigs, remnants of the last storm. They did not speak, so Missy thought he might still be mad at her. She also thought she heard him talking to someone early Thursday morning, but she did not put her eyes on him. "I think I heard him talking to someone—it wasn't a very long conversation, just a few sentences," she explained. "I wasn't really paying attention but right after that I heard the beep of a golf cart backing up, and then it pulled forward right out of the driveway. I heard the tires on the gravel. I assumed it was him but I didn't see him—could have been someone who sounded like him, like a visitor to the lighthouse who left when it wasn't open. I'm just not—well, I'm not sure what else there is to say."

"Did you hear any part of the conversation on Thursday? Anything at all? Any words or phrases?" Barb asked.

"I was only half listening," she said, looking up, her eyes filling again with tears. "I was so mad at him for the way he had dropped me, I didn't want to hear if he was talking to Theresa or some other woman. He may have said something about a plan or the plan—something like that, maybe? I assumed whoever was talking was making plans and those plans did not include me."

She looked directly at us and I could tell she was angry again. Relationships are never easy, I thought to myself—no matter what the relationship is.

Chapter 9

On Sunday, I woke up exhausted, feeling like sleep was a missed opportunity. Yesterday had been a draining day and my mind just didn't shut off last night. I looked over at the beautiful view from my bedroom window and my eyes went to the empty dog bed, which jolted me awake.

"Buddy?" I called and I felt the soft thump of his tail. The small black donut was on the end of my bed. "What are you doing, mister?" There is nothing better for soothing your mood than the steadiness of a dog.

Before long, we were on our way to Books & Brew. The crowd, if we were lucky enough to have one, would arrive later in the day, after church, after checkouts and check-ins and after the ferries started arriving. So, I intended to enjoy the quiet time, tackling the work from yesterday. There was some inventory to put out and I wanted to give the store a good cleaning while no one was there. Buddy was happy to settle into one of the comfy club chairs and supervise my work.

I was carrying the events from yesterday with me as I worked. My arms felt heavy and my back was tight. After three or four things were crossed off my list, I knew the only way I could start processing what happened was to put my pen to paper and map out all I had learned. So, Buddy and I sat together, each lost in our own thoughts. It was very likely both of us had Carl on our minds.

"Carl? Are you in here, hello?" I heard Barb calling from the porch and we went to greet her.

"Hey, Barb! Come in." I smiled, already feeling better now that I put my eyes on her. She looked unrested, too, but overall, she seemed to mentally be in a better place than yesterday. "I purposely did not call you today, I was hoping you could sleep in a little."

"Not much sleep for me, I'm afraid," she said, "But I ate well last night and sat on my porch. I think maybe some part of the shock has worn off, a little at least."

I told her what I had been up to before she arrived and handed her my notebook with all of yesterday's events recorded in it. She read all of it quickly and said, "I really had no idea Missy and Carl were a thing. Never saw them together once!"

I went to make us some tea and listened to Barb's suggestion of how we should handle the situation in which we now found ourselves. "We both know this is a small community," she said. "People will find out we were the ones who discovered Carl and there will be lots of questions, lots of theories, and lots of rumors. We needed to decide what we are willing to say—which at this point is pretty easy because we don't really know much."

Deputy Julie's promise of touching base soon was hanging over us. The more we knew, the harder it was going to be to keep our neighbors and friends at arm's length.

Barb finally said what we both were thinking: "If there is a murderer here, we need to protect ourselves and each other."

"I'm so impulsive, I wish I never said anything about getting those pictures. I wish I never brought this to our door. I'm sorry Barb, I am sorry for making you a part of this. You know, when Rob and I would argue, sometimes it bothered him that I jumped in or said something without thinking it through. Now, instead of Rob, it's you who has to deal with my mess. I hate that I did this to you."

After several moments of searching the depth of her teacup, Barb looked up. "You don't honestly believe all that nonsense, do you? I mean, come on, you didn't make me go to Governor's Point, I wanted to! I love it there but I'm always distracted and running around, who knows if I would have even noticed the gate? And it's just not true that you dumped a 'mess' on me. My life is always chaos, hurrying here, hurrying there. When you live alone, you don't have anyone point out your quirks and I guess mine are getting worse with age. I've lived alone a long time since Danny left. I don't think you're as impulsive as you think you are, I think you put other people first—but you know what you want. When you finally see a chance to do it, you go for it. I don't accept your apology, you didn't do anything wrong." She smiled so kindly, I felt the sting of tears.

It was this and all the other interactions like this that smoothed out the sharp edges of my heart that had emerged since Rob's death. I know I was more aware of it because the anniversary of his death was here.

Barb somehow sensed what I was thinking. She continued, "And I bet if Rob was sitting in that chair right there, he would say that he did his own fair share of knucklehead things. Carr, you have to be careful not to make him into some kind of a saint. He was a wonderful man and a great father, but he wasn't perfect either, like the rest of us." She shifted in her seat, brushed invisible crumbs from her legs, and said, "You keep doing you! You're good for us here on our quirky island. We will figure all this out—together."

I wasn't sure how she did it but I felt one hundred pounds lighter when she was done talking. "Even when you're calling me out, you still make me feel like a champ," I laughed, and she laughed with me.

"That's just my special gift," she said.

The parade of golf carts riding by told me church services were over and Tripp soon arrived. He reported there were quite a few neighbors who had questions for him about what he knew from our experience yesterday. Barb and I looked knowingly at each other. We definitely were going to have to really figure out how we would handle this.

"By the way, Helen said the book club was going to have their meeting here tomorrow, sometime early afternoon. Sound good?" Tripp said.

It didn't, but I was not interested in explaining why I was trying to have a low-key day tomorrow.

"Hmm, how about moving her group to Tuesday, Tripp? I can get them one of Miss Lucy's pies and set them up right. I expect a big delivery of books tomorrow and I would rather not be unpacking, sorting, pricing, you know, doing all that stuff, with the ladies here. Can you call Helen and see if Tuesday works for her group?"

He agreed and hopefully so would Helen.

As promised, Deputy Julie paid us a visit. She clearly had not been affected by the sleep issues Barb and I shared. Julie began the conversation with confirmation from the morgue that the victim was Coastal Carl. It wasn't any easier to hear the news for the second time. As she spoke, I took notes and, when she paused, I told her about Missy's memory that Carl may have left the lighthouse on Thursday for his final time.

"That fits the timeline. The coroner will have the blood and all the other lab reports tomorrow afternoon, but from the physical analysis, I can tell you now that Carl did not drown. His lungs had no water in them. Unfortunately, he had pretty substantial intracranial hemorrhaging, which seems to have been caused by impact from a flat surfaced object." She flipped her curls over one shoulder and watched for my reaction.

"So, he was hit on the head and then somehow fell into the pool?" I responded, probably louder than I should have, as it suddenly was noticeably quieter in the room. Julie said nothing. I moved to the porch and felt everyone's eyes on me as Julie followed.

"Julie, look, I came here to Mongin Island to escape the feeling like impending doom was hanging over my head. I want to help you. I want to do something for Carl, he deserved better than this. It has only been a day, but I swear it feels like it has already been a month of this, of not knowing what happened or who did it, you know?"

"A hundred percent, I get it. There is something in your world now that never was before and look, if you want to help, I am not going to refuse it. Not being right there in the community is definitely going to slow the pieces coming together. The biggest help will be talking to people who may know something. They trust you, and you may have access I don't. Will you do that? The notes you took with Missy, the things you noticed all were helpful—really helpful."

With that, we made a plan that I would gather my information and email her my notes daily. We scheduled a brief call twice a day and I got to work. The structure of a project and the idea of working toward a goal were the guardrails I needed to feel the chaos could be contained. I felt a little lighter, in a small way.

When I walked back into the shop, I felt like all eyes were still on me, but I got busy with my to-do list, which so far had not received all that much attention. Tripp had the shelves polished and the glass doors and windows cleaned. I really appreciated him doing that heavy, physical work. The salt in the air coated the windows and doors. Sand found its way in the door even at this distance from the beach. Everything seemed brighter already, but island living did require never-ending maintenance.

While I looked around for my next task, I noticed a familiar tall presence in the non-fiction section. Paul Easton was back, as he had promised. Immediately, my impulse was to pretend I hadn't seen him. What was it about this man that was so draining? Best to just get it over with, I thought, moving to his side.

"Good morning, Paul. How's your Sunday going?"

"My Sunday is likely off to a better start than yours, I would surmise. Good morning to you, Carr. Awful circumstances you found yourself in yesterday, as the story presumably goes," he said as he turned toward me. He was perfectly dressed in light wool gabardine pants, cuffed with polished leather loafers. His golf polo was tucked in at the waist and his brown leather concho belt caught my eye. Again, his formality was not in step with the usual visitors' wardrobe. How did he manage to keep his clothing, right down to his shoes, so immaculately spotless and wrinkle free on an island where sand and salt are drawn like metal to magnets and everyone sweats?

"Yesterday certainly wasn't the day we intended, that's for sure," I said. "Terrible thing for Carl and for all of us. I'm sorry I wasn't more available to you yesterday. How can I help you?"

He was a mystery to me, he had only been cordial and yet, there was something so off-putting about him, something that made me immediately defensive and guarded.

"Well, looking at your stock, I may be somewhat premature. But I was wondering—since you are now the sole bookseller on our island—whether you plan to deal in rare books."

"Rare books? I'm just getting my connections with wholesalers organized to carry current titles—and in the back room, we're dealing in used books. But rare books are a part of the business I had not necessarily decided to pursue." Then, I realized that I could at least consider expanding the business. So, I began with another: "But—we are a historic island and perhaps there's a market here."

"Perhaps," he said, pulling a small leather-covered notebook from his pocket. "I actually have a few titles I would be interested in purchasing if you could help me track them down."

"You couldn't find them online? That's usually everyone's first stop these days."

"No, I have tried. I was thinking you might—through your distributors perhaps—have access to some networks of dealers as a bookseller yourself, you know. You might make inquiries? Find a range of prices?"

"I'm just thinking other stores, or other people with more established networks may be more helpful to you. I don't want to waste your time."

"While other shops have certainly verbalized interest in finding these books, none have been successful. My research awaits and in fact, I was thrilled to learn your establishment opened and coincided with my annual visit."

"I could try," I said, taking a slip of paper he offered from his notebook with several titles he had neatly listed in black pen.

As I was studying his list, he said, "Mongin Island has a very rich history, as I am sure you, a woman of great intellect, already know, correct? Yet it is hard to separate fact from lore, isn't that so?"

I nodded, but he apparently did not expect an answer, because he went on: "I have spent many years studying this region and the role this island played in the founding of your country. Although some may call me an expert, and I do so appreciate their confidence, clearly, I do still have a few unanswered questions. This brings me to you." He smiled, briefly, which was not at all comforting. His smile seemed forced, and these comments felt rehearsed. Nothing about him seemed authentic, unplanned, or spontaneous.

I found myself trying to figure out what he wasn't saying versus what he actually did say. I said, "Of course, we all know of the island's role in both the Revolutionary War and the Civil War. But tell me a little more about these books you want. One of these titles seems to be about the coast before the Revolutionary War. What's your project?"

"A valid question indeed. It is the Revolutionary War that is of particular interest to me. Certainly, we are on opposite sides of that one, but we can still be friends." He laughed slightly. I was convinced now that he had rehearsed this whole presentation. "That era and the colonial era before that are my current field of study."

"And you really couldn't find these books yourself? With all your research and your own contacts? To be honest, I would have to start from scratch myself," I said. Clearly, I knew little about this side of the business. I was beginning to think there were catches in this offer that I could not foresee. "This isn't an expertise I had planned to develop for the store."

"Well, please consider it, because this is potentially lucrative for you and well, in this case, for me. To locate these particular books, you are probably going to have to reach out to rare book collectors who—I must confess—I've found to be impossible fortune hunters! I've made my own inquiries but was thinking that a third party—a new book-seller like yourself—might want to help a potential loyal customer. I would imagine that dealers would love to make the acquaintance of someone with a serious inquiry with some potentially big payoffs for them. This is a good way to help me and of course, help yourself. May I implore you to help me? I would be forever in your debt."

"Okay, let's sit down and make a few notes," I said and ushered Paul to the big table on our Trading Floor. We sat down once more to go over his list. It turned out Paul had done extensive research on the wars fought in and around our island and he was happy to share many of the highlights. He had facts and figures on the societal, economic, and policy effects of many battles, including the three pre-Revolutionary War conflicts fought on Mongin Island.

"You are aware that the Spanish, who were part of the European colonization of this island, did not want us, the English, so close to all their settlements in Florida? You know this, I assume. They encouraged Native American tribes to attack our colonists. Sadly for those Native Americans, they lost all three battles, and unfortunately for you, they helped to foster a British stronghold here, ready to fight the American colonists just a few years later. This is likely not part of your educational narrative, I presume. The English who settled here in that era were a force, I say!" Paul exclaimed, his voice growing stronger with pride as he got to the end of this history lesson. His eyes were wide, his face was red, and stared at me with an intensity that caused me to back up a little.

I was both impressed and leery of his request. "That is a part of our island's history many people may not fully appreciate or understand," I said. "I think most people are aware that Mongin was part of both the Revolutionary and Civil Wars, but I don't think people know these details. Would you be interested in doing a presentation on this topic, here at the store? I think people would like to learn more and we could schedule a casual get-together one evening. I know for many of us, we didn't cover these smaller battles in school and think about the Revolutionary War as more of a northern battle, you know: Boston Tea Party and all." I thought Paul would love the opportunity to be the subject matter expert with a captive audience.

The spell was broken and Paul was back to some kind of a character in community theater. "How very kind of you to humor me," he said as he smoothed his hair and straightened his shoulders into his rod-straight posture. "I am unfortunately otherwise engaged and cannot offer my services in this capacity."

I seemed to have failed some kind of test I didn't realize I was taking.

"No, honestly, I think—" I started.

He cut me off. "It is just that I only have a matter of weeks on the island this time and I am determined to complete this phase of my research as soon as possible. I have been stalled at this impasse for far too long. I came in today hoping to establish a good working relationship with you. I truly am pleased you've opened this establishment and I wish you well. I thought my request might be as favorable to you as it will be to me."

"Certainly, and this idea is—definitely intriguing. I have a lot on my plate right now, but I will do my best."

"Well, if you can perhaps find the time to pursue this sleuthing for me, in the very near future, I do want to emphasize that there should be a financially beneficial gem or two on this list—from your perspective, I mean, in terms of your own fees."

"I would be happy to try."

"Thank you," he said, rising. "And I do not want to impose on your kindness much longer. You certainly have been most attentive to me. As I have explained, I realize that these books are not easily available. Some were published as small print runs by regional printer-binders that are long gone. They never made it into library collections. I'm laying out a real challenge here for you."

"As I said, my relationships with my distributors are all new. I can certainly ask them, on your behalf, about these books. Of course, I will do that for you, Paul, but I can't promise great results. I just don't have a lot of well-established professional connections yet and I have been purchasing mostly commercial runs. I'm fully admitting that rare books would be a brand-new venture for me." Suddenly, I was more nervous than I had been in weeks, rattling on about our agreement, repeating myself, hoping to make this clear to him.

"I do understand," he said, rather coldly. "There are several critically important concerns I have. I cannot emphasize enough the magnitude of the decisions I am making where information from these volumes will contribute to this analysis. I need these books. Do your best, please, and I will reward you for your efforts. I can assure you of that. You have my word."

I promised I would start the search later that day. With a slight bow and a smile, he said, "I bid you a pleasant day."

Once he was gone, I returned to stocking with Tripp and wondered exactly what Paul Easton was working on that was so mission-critical in relation to these obscure historical texts.

What I discovered that day Paul visited Books & Brew is that my customers were quickly proving to be as fascinating as the volumes on my shelves.

Chapter 10

Barb left shortly after Paul as she had several guests arriving and properties that needed inspection. Tripp was busy trimming back some of the tall grasses that framed our walkway. Business was steady in the store and the waves of people kept my focus on the present. My day was filled with some of my regulars and a good mix of new faces, some just on Mongin Island for the day. After the afternoon rush, I paused to look around the shop that I had brought to life. The sun had already done its work for the day and was on the other half of its job. There was still a lot of natural light in the room, but it was now a gentle glow, as if everything was in its proper place. The room was warm, not by temperature, but by feeling. It was as if, at this moment, everything was exactly as it was supposed to be.

With renewed energy, I thought I would start emailing my contacts regarding Paul's request. I gathered my laptop and his list and started outside to the rockers. On my way through the store, my eyes went to Buddy and his new friend, a child who looked about 10 years old, snugly sitting in one of the club chairs. He reminded me of my Nicholas, with medium brown hair and a sun-freckled nose. The tips of his tennis shoes did not quite touch the floor. He had a couple of scabs on his knees and shins, a likely homage to days playing a sport or riding a bike. The boy's head was bent into *Charlie Bone and the Red Knight* and Buddy was curled into his usual donut position, with his head resting on this boy's leg.

"I see you met our mascot, Buddy," I said, smiling at my young customer.

"He is awesome," the boy replied. "He hopped up with me. Is that okay?" He looked worried.

"It's more than okay," I reassured him. "It's wonderful you are so nice to him. He has had a lot of change recently and he might be missing a good friend of his. Dogs are a good judge of character and it looks like Buddy chose you to be his friend."

In the span of a few minutes, I learned Jacob just moved to Mongin Island. His mom was enrolling him in the island school and had given him a few dollars to spend as he waited.

"Your principal loves island families and is so excited for a new student, she opened the school on Sunday to get you registered! I bet you will love your new school. I am really glad to meet you and I know Buddy is, too. Summer vacation will be here soon. What would you think about coming to a reading group, here in the store, every now and then? I am thinking about having some events like that for readers like you."

He frowned a little and said, "I don't think I can. My mom will be working at the resort and I don't think, well—I am not sure we can buy books right now."

"Well, sometimes people like to trade books. I have a whole room just for trades. How about if I make you a deal? If you read that Charlie Bone book, come and tell me about it. If your mom agrees, you can pick a few more things that look interesting from the Trading Floor. Someday, you may have a few things to drop off, but for now, you can pick whatever you like and maybe talk about it with other readers your own age. How does that sound?"

He bit his bottom lip, just like Nicholas used to when he didn't know what to say. "I don't think I have enough money to buy this book." He looked up so sadly. In this simple exchange, another puzzle piece of my mission clicked into place. I wanted to share my love of reading, and here was the perfect candidate. Like Allen a few months before, Jacob gave me the gift of this opportunity, this ability to share what I love in a place that I love.

"I understand that. Sometimes we don't have enough money to buy everything we may like. I'll tell you what, you take this book and read it. When you are done, come and tell me about it. How does that sound? Please give your mom this card." I handed him one. "It has my name and how to reach me. She and I can talk about my idea and if it doesn't work out, that's okay too. I just wanted to thank you for being so nice to Buddy when he needed a friend. It was really nice to meet you, and thank you for visiting my store. You are welcome here any time! Oh, and welcome to Mongin Island, Jacob! There are quite a few people around your age who live here, too. Before you know it, you are going to have some new friends, I am absolutely sure of it."

Jacob slowly stood up, gently moving Buddy's head. "Thank you for the book. Yes, I'd like to come back here. I wasn't able to bring my old collection so this will be the first book here in my new room." He looked up shyly and then hugged me quickly. If I learned anything from being the mother of a boy, it was to relish these spontaneous, heartfelt displays of emotion.

"Jacob, you are very welcome. I am looking forward to seeing you again, hopefully soon."

"I am going to tell my mom all about this place. She will be happy, I know it." He smiled at me and then curled back up in his chair. Buddy readjusted himself and the two were once again blissfully enjoying each other.

As I settled myself on the porch with my laptop and Paul's list, I sent emails marked with the red high priority exclamation point to all my book contacts. All I could do was wait for their responses.

I started thinking about how to help Julie. What should my next step be? I noticed a young woman with shoulder length blonde hair walking quickly toward the store. She had a canvas bag with a long strap over her shoulder and was dressed in a long sleeve shirt and a windbreaker.

"Can I help you?" I asked as she climbed the stairs.

"I am here to pick up my son. I asked him to wait for me here," she said, her voice flat and without any emotion. She continued up the stairs, almost entering the store before I could introduce myself. "You must be Jacob's mom. I am Carr. This is my place. It is wonderful to meet you."

She looked at me sharply, "I'm Katie. Was he causing you a problem? I told him to just sit quietly. He won't be bothering you anymore."

"Bothering me? Certainly not! He was one of the highlights of my day. I gave him a card that I asked him to give to you so we could meet and talk. You have a lovely, well-behaved, boy there. Would you like to come in and have a cup of tea with me?"

"You want to have a cup of tea with me?"

"Yes, I would love to, and please, let me show you my shop. I hope you and Jacob will spend some time here. He told me you will be working at the resort, so maybe when your schedule allows, you can come to events here and meet some of your neighbors."

I held the door open for her and, as she walked through, she said, "My neighbors? I'm working in housekeeping. We live in the employee housing on the resort property. I don't have neighbors."

I smiled at her, "Yes you do. We are all your neighbors. I only live about three streets away from you. I live on the resort property, too. Would you like some peppermint tea?" We walked into the main room, where she saw Jacob and Buddy in the chair together.

"Hi, Mom! Come meet Buddy!" he said excitedly. Katie walked over to Jacob and ran her fingers through his hair. She looked over at me and I saw the first glimpse of a smile. We were getting somewhere. "Come make yourself at home at this big table in this room. I will bring the tea."

My last two customers were ready to check out. I quickly rang them up, made our tea and walked back to Katie. "It's a good time to talk. It's just the four of us now: you, Jacob, Buddy, and me," I said as I brought our mugs to the table.

As she sipped from her cup, I thought I would take the first step in swapping our island arrival stories. I focused mine on how Meredith and Nicholas had enjoyed their time on the island as children when they were Jacob's age. I couldn't help but share how much Jacob reminded me of Nicholas and offered my own opinion that as moms, we have to look out for each other's children. I tried to be as reassuring as I could. I paused between anecdotes, not wanting to overwhelm her but hoping she might volunteer her own story.

Finally, Katie reciprocated, guardedly at first, but then more and more openly: She had Jacob when she was just a teenager, desperately trying to escape the wrath of an abusive father and uncle in southern California. Her family was broken in so many ways and she knew she could never raise a child there. Jacob's father ended up in prison before her son was born, which meant she had to work night and day to carve out a safe life for the boy. She bounced through a long list of menial jobs in that region, always moving on if she felt Jacob was at risk in any way. She intentionally started looking for job postings on the Atlantic coast when Jacob's father finally got out of jail and began stalking her. She actually came to the area to work on the mainland because it's such a tourist spot, with lots of hotels and restaurants that were always hiring.

"But someone else had directed me here to Mongin. I heard some people can hide here, without a bridge and all. Makes it easier to not be found, if you don't want to be. Then I took the ferry over one day—and I was sold. I want my son to know the stability I never had. I want him to be someplace where he can just be a kid," she said. "If I watch my budget, we can make it here. And I've got talents. My job is housekeeping for now, but I can move up here. I can see that plain as day."

Our tea was gone. I collected her cup as I said, "You know, school's out soon and I wouldn't mind having Jacob around the bookstore for some book clubs or events. There are many island children who are good readers. I have been working with the school to plan some events for the children. I want to do a summer reading program, or something like that."

Katie was silent for a moment. "Jacob has never been invited anywhere, really. This is really quite amazing. Thank you. He will be in the summer camp the resort provides for the employees' families. But

I know he will want to wander over here after camp or on the weekends. It's close enough that he can walk from the resort to this shop. Since the roads aren't busy, I know he can do it. Please, you have to tell me if he doesn't behave or if he steps out of line."

"Wonderful, Katie! I definitely will let you know if we have any bumps along the way, but I am not expecting that. And, I will also let you know when we see the good things that I really think Jacob will do. I think this will be a great summer. I hope so, anyway."

Katie finally broke out a broad smile. "I hope he makes some friends and finally doesn't have to worry about moving, packing up in the middle of the night and leaving without ever saying goodbye to anyone."

It was such a simple hope for a mother to have for her child. She just wanted her son to be home.

"Katie, before you go, look around the Trading Floor and see if there is anything in here that interests you. I am about ready to close up and head home. Can I give you guys a ride?"

"That would be great, but let me clean up these mugs, at least," she said, quietly.

"Absolutely not, you pick something from here and I will shut off the lights and gather our boys—one fuzzy one and one freckled one! Be back in a minute."

Just a few minutes later, we piled into my cart—all of us heading home.

Chapter 11

Early on Monday, I took Buddy for a long walk on the beach. He wasn't a big fan of the water even though he clearly had some Labrador retriever in his DNA and usually Labs love a good swim. He did like to walk on the sand and sniff at the treasures we found along the way. I walked closest to the waves and liked the numbing feeling of the cold water on my feet. I wanted to be numb, not to feel today, the day I had been dreading for months. I needed this time to myself. I needed this beach, this scene, to fortify me for today. It was the anniversary of Rob's death.

Anniversary seemed like the ultimate misnomer. There would be no more anniversaries, no more celebrations of us. It was really a statement, a marker that "we" didn't exist anymore. All of the firsts—the holidays, the birthdays, and the milestones without him—had happened and they were all painful cycles of anticipation, disappointment, sadness, and steps forward. Now, on this final first, I knew the drill, the plan for the day. I would get through it and push forward, no matter how imperfectly and awkwardly, no matter how impossible it seemed. Meredith, Nicholas, and I had scheduled a video call for tonight and had planned to share our favorite Rob stories, ones that would help us celebrate the wonderful, patient, smart, and loyal man he was. I just needed to get through the rest of the day until then, hold it together for a dozen or so more hours.

When I got to the store, Helen was sitting on the front steps waiting for me. "So, book club tomorrow? Did I hear you say something about a pie?" she greeted me.

"Good news travels fast, doesn't it?" I smiled as I searched my bag for the store keys.

"Miss Lucy is supposedly trying a new recipe—well, at least that's what she told some of the ladies—so we are ready to take you up on your offer! Very kind of you, Carr, thank you," she said. "I also wanted to let you know that the tourism board is coming to the island today. I think there are a dozen or so travel writers, event planners, and people like that who will be touring around today. I think Suzanne put Books & Brew on the tour. Did anyone reach out to you?"

"No, I didn't know anything about that, but I will be ready. Thanks for the heads up. This is exactly the kind of grassroots marketing I can use. How great for Mongin Island!" I said.

"It's terrible timing, if you ask me, what with a murder here? It couldn't be worse! I just hope Suzanne keeps them moving and no one decides to make this the focal point of the visit. Which, by the way: I know you know what happened. So, what can you tell me?"

"Helen, I really don't know much. I just happened to be—"

"If you ask me, I think Missy is hiding something," she interrupted. "She spent the last few weeks telling Suzanne that Carl was going to propose to her and how she hoped he would sell the lighthouse and move back to Maine with her, where there are real lighthouses. I mean, have you heard of anything so ridiculous? He wasn't a lighthouse keeper! He was a real estate agent who lived in a house with a big light in it. Ridiculous! Carl Tibbons living and operating a lighthouse? He made millions over the years through all the development on this island selling properties. Carl would never move."

"Millions? He was that successful?"

"Okay, well, maybe not millions, but a lot of money definitely." She stood up and continued, "In fact, he sold some properties several times over through the highs and lows here. Carl was often the agent on both sides of the sale, so he had done very well for himself. I know for a fact that he also did some trades, you know, swapping one piece of land for another. Shoot, he even swapped a lot way down by the county dock for a full house on Old Port Passage Way. That man would do anything for a deal. Don't get me wrong, he worked hard, he hustled for his success. He had the gift of gab, that's for sure and maybe he just told Missy what she wanted to hear—but I think she knows a lot more about this than she is saying. She definitely saw a future for them and I guess Carl did not."

I was now very curious about Missy. "It seemed like Carl lived kind of modestly. I mean his house was nice, but not extravagant. Do you think Missy knew how well he had done in real estate? He certainly didn't seem to be showy or anything. Would she know this if she hadn't been on the island long?"

"She's been here long enough to know this, if this is the kind of thing that is important to you," Helen said, leaving no doubt that she was going to tell me more of her Missy theory. As I opened the shop, Helen sat in a club chair and told me about the interactions with Missy she and other book club ladies had over the last month or so, which all seemed to point to a very different person than the Missy I met. Helen's lengthy list of examples of Missy's relationship goals, long term plans, and wish list of expensive gift ideas were describing a side of Missy I had not observed.

My head was filled with so many different things—Rob, my kids, Carl, Governor's Point, Paul, and antique books. I didn't have the capacity to absorb all these seemingly unrelated stories.

Finally, I cut her off. "I have to say, Helen, I didn't see this side of Missy. Granted, we were talking under very different and strange circumstances. I don't know what to think. I had the unfortunate task of telling her about Carl and then, of course, she was already rattled because she found us wandering around Carl's house. Maybe if I had met her under different circumstances, on a different day, maybe I would have picked up on some of these same things you're saying, but I didn't get any of this from her."

"Well, something doesn't add up to me, that's what I do know." Helen stood up and said, "I will leave you to your work. Tripp said you were expecting a large delivery on the barge today and the travel group is on the 10 a.m. ferry, so they could likely be here before lunch, or maybe even right after, depending on the route Suzanne decides to take. Looking forward to pie tomorrow at the book club! We will see you here and I guess we will grab the table on the Trading Floor. I am going to head over to The Tin Drum now. I wonder if they know to expect a crowd of influencers. You know how it is at that shop. They're iron artists. They might be in the middle of some custom work there and have all the tools out—not exactly welcoming! I love Suzanne but I had hoped she would have told all our retailers to put out the welcome mat for this group. I mean, if she wants to serve as our rep for the County Tourism Committee, she needs to take things more seriously. She should be a better communicator!" She continued with her *tsk, tsking* as she climbed into her cart.

"Wow, that was a lot," I thought as I watched her drive away. Helen's suspicions, the stories, and the pictures they painted weighed on me, so I recorded these details in my notebook and decided to update Julie. Helen raised a good point. What if there was more to Missy's reactions than I first thought?

Tripp and I were soon diving into our new inventory. We worked in silent harmony, each person knowing exactly what to do, and just doing it. We were two hands on a keyboard. It was so easy to work with Tripp; I made a mental note to thank him when we were done. We were on such a roll that I hated to break the workflow.

But as Helen predicted, the tourism group arrived before lunch and their excited voices immediately filled the store. They were a lively group, interested in learning about my road to becoming a retailer, my connection to the island, and how I would contribute to the overall Mongin Island experience. My story was easy to tell: I loved this place and although independent bookstores faced pressure from online retailers, this store was different because it was becoming part of the community. Happily, this was a place people were coming to meet their friends, catch up on the day, and maybe buy or trade a book.

Even better, business was brisk! The group essentially bought out the entire section of Mongin Island books, including a new book of poetry I had unpacked moments before their arrival.

Julie walked through the door just as I was saying goodbye to the group. They posed for a picture on the front porch, filling up the rockers, and were bantering about what hashtags they would use in their social media posts. With smiles and waves, they were off to the next stop. A few other customers were sitting around the shop, so Julie and I found a quiet space in my office to talk privately. Julie's team had been collecting evidence at Governor's Point and Carl's house. They had spoken to Missy and were in contact with Theresa, so I shared Helen's feedback.

"Interesting, definitely a twist," Julie said, as I warmed up her tea. "What was your vibe about Missy? We are checking into her story about dating Carl and seeing what else we can find out about her, but it is an interesting theory about her wanting to move away with Carl. All this feedback seems to suggest that Missy has a lot of emotion and energy invested in Carl. Very interesting."

"I am not sure how much I am believing Helen's gossip," I said. "I want to talk to Missy again with a clearer head. Saturday, I mean, it was just too much going on for someone like me who doesn't do this all day. I told her we would stay in touch."

"Before you do, let's go over the list of things we collected. I want you to have some context and understand where I think this is headed." She gave me an inventory list of items the team had collected. Among these was Carl's laptop. Julie said the lock-screen password was written on a sticky note on the corner of the machine, next to the mousepad. "Why bother even having a password?" Julie gave me a look. "Certainly makes our job easy, but—"

"I guess anyone with access to Carl's house could also have had access to his files. On second thought, not just his house, right? This laptop could have traveled with him, too," I said, half to Julie and half to myself. Would Carl have taken it to real estate showings, open houses, and customer meetings? "Could you tell if his files were password protected?"

"We didn't get there yet, but I am bringing it back to the mainland for us to examine more closely. Sheriff Oxley is trying to get us some forensic accounting help. Our main resource has been out sick for the last week and his backup is involved in that big case in the news, the one with the lawyer from the city who hired someone to kill his family. I don't think anyone is going to be able to start on this until tomorrow at the earliest."

"I'm no forensic expert, that's for sure, but I have done a lot of financial analysis for my clients," I said.

Julie was smiling.

"You were going to ask me already, weren't you?"

"Well, I did come here today thinking—you know, maybe I can get a little more help from you?"

"I definitely can look into this," I said, "but I know you need to maintain a record of all of this, right? Anything you might find that you'd want to use in court will have to be verified. You don't want people tampering with the laptop."

"Chain of custody, right. We've got to be careful."

"Hmm, can someone on your team provide me access to the files on his computer in a data room? That's what we use at my firm. That's a way to maintain the integrity of the data. We're always conscious of being sued about sensitive records, so we use a data vault so no opposing counsel can claim we manipulated data."

"Data vault, okay." Now Julie was making a note. "I knew you had the skills. Email me the specs of what you want so our IT guys can set this up for you. We do use some software like what you're describing. I will get this set up—and send you the login. Your help would be amazing. I am still going to see what forensic accounting help Sheriff Oxley can find, but in full transparency, Carr, I just don't think this case is going to be a big priority for Oxley."

"I'm happy to help. This is something I can do and I can likely do it pretty quickly."

"I'm glad you understand how urgent this is. People aren't going to rest, thinking there is a killer on the loose. It's bad for tourism too, I know. Small community like this, everyone is aware of what is happening. It's not good." Julie's smile was gone.

Julie finished reviewing the evidence cataloged so far and agreed to provide an updated list by tomorrow. Talking theory, Julie seemed to think Carl had been at home, was called away, and somehow got to Governor's Point, where he was hit on the head with a rock and ultimately was pushed into the pool.

"That can't be it," I said. "I mean that can't be the whole story. We think Carl left the lighthouse on Thursday. If he drove to Governor's Point, then where is his cart? It wasn't there and Missy feels reasonably confident that he did drive away then. I mean, his cart isn't at his house and his cart isn't at Governor's Point. So where is his cart? That's what we need to find. On an island this size, we should be able to find something like that, right? And find it quickly?"

"Ha, well, you would think so, but so many of these golf carts look identical. When you talk to Missy, see if she can remember anything particular about Carl's cart. Did Carl have a bumper sticker or something, anything unique on his? Did you see that cart with the Georgia Bulldog on the hood? Now, only if we could get that lucky with Carl's! Instead, I bet we are looking for an off-white four-seater!"

Sadly, I had to agree. Julie essentially described my cart—and at least half of the other ones on the island. No wonder there were frequently cases of mistaken identities, with people driving off in the wrong cart, especially because many keys fit multiple carts. Same manufacturer, often the same key.

"One more thing, Carr. It looks like Carl traveled recently, right? Seems like he was meeting with someone in New York, Newport, Rhode Island, and someplace out by the Outer Banks. From what I can tell, it seems like it may be the same person or people in all of those places. You know anything about this?"

"No, nothing specific," I replied. "He told me about travel. That's how I ended up with Buddy. He said he needed to be flexible around someone else's schedule and needed help with Buddy's care."

"Well, one common name showing up in all these places is Evan Weisman. Mean anything to you?"

"Unfortunately, no, but I will keep my eyes open when I get into Carl's files."

"Tripp, are you okay if I scoot out for a little bit?" I asked as Julie and I walked to the front of the store. "I have a few things I need to do. I know I am leaving you with a few more boxes to unload, so don't worry if you can't get to them. Just do what you can—and the rest will wait. I will be in the store early tomorrow and can finish whatever we don't get to today."

I continued talking as I walked out the door and called "Thanks! See you soon!" to him and whoever else was listening. I didn't give him a chance to ask any questions, which I hoped would stop people from pumping him for details he did not have.

As I drove, I organized my thoughts, trying to categorize facts versus theories. Following the music coming from the back of Missy's house, I found her sitting on her deck, a book on her lap but her eyes looking off into the distance.

"Missy, hey, how are you today? I wanted to catch up with you. Do you have a minute?"

Her eyes focused on me but she did not seem to really see me for a minute or so. "Carr, sorry, sure, yes, sit down here." She waved to the selection of deck chairs scattered around in no particular way. "I was a thousand miles away."

There were quite a few things I wanted to ask Missy, but if I learned anything from time on Mongin Island, it was that some conversations were like a Georgia-milled carpet, all rolled up. When installing that carpet, you start in one corner of the room and you better only unroll a little at a time. If you moved too fast, you would end up in a big mess. So, I took a deep breath, settled into my chair, and waited for Missy. We covered the easy things, the weather, the tourists and day-trippers heading to the beach, and then she asked about the investigation. I felt the tug of that carpet, the pull of the next section ready to be moved into place.

"Julie told me that they collected a lot of things from Carl's house," I said, keeping my voice steady. "Things like his computer, some files, and what looks like his pocket calendar where a lot of appointments and notes were kept. Her team is going through all that they collected from here and from Governor's Point."

"I don't know much about what he kept in that pocket diary. I think he mostly wrote things in it when he was out and about, like if someone asked him to call them later or mentioned a tip, or something. You know you can't always get wireless here—you have to face the ocean to get a good signal. I don't think he kept his laptop with him unless he was at an appointment, but I don't know, I really never paid that much attention to it." She answered simply and I believed her.

"Did you ever use his laptop? Do you know how he organized his files?"

"Of course I didn't," she snapped. "Why would I need his computer?"

"You know, if you were together and wanted to look up something, or print something, check your email, whatever, a million reasons. So, you didn't ever use it?"

"No, never, I never touched it. Not one time. We didn't have that kind of a relationship." She shook her head and stood up. I wondered about the "kind of relationship" you needed to use someone else's computer but, in the meantime, her statement opened the door for me to explore her perspective on the kind of relationship they did have. "So, you weren't very close then?" I ventured, wondering if she was about to walk into her house and not finish this conversation.

Missy eyed me up and down. She looked at me like she was seeing me for the first time. "I told you that we were seeing each other and then he started seeing Theresa. Does that sound like we were very close? I mean, he dropped me over his dog. Remember? Doesn't exactly sound like I was the love of his life, right? No, we weren't very close."

"I know it's painful, Missy. And I'm sorry to bring up something you might find a little humiliating." We sat with that statement in the air between us for a few minutes. "You're essentially telling me how Carl felt, but what about how you felt? Did you see a future for the two of you? You lived right next to each other, you must have spent a lot of time together."

I realized I was playing with the charms on my bracelet. Each one of them meant something. Friendship, good wishes, appreciation. My Atlanta book club friends gave me this bracelet when I moved and I very rarely took it off because it reminded me of some very happy times we shared. My left hand was mindlessly twirling the charms around the band. If Missy noticed this, she would have seen that this conversation was difficult for me too.

"What are you saying? You're saying I was a fool? I already know that," she said, eventually. She sat down again, but this time in a different chair. She chose a seat closer to me, so our crossed legs were practically touching.

"No! I am just asking—" I started, shifting in my seat.

"No, okay? No, I didn't think we would be together forever, but I didn't think it would end like this." Her hair was pulled up into a ponytail and I could see the color rise through her neck and onto her face. "I really hadn't thought that much about anything. We were just getting to really know each other." She looked over my shoulder, her line of sight focused right on Carl's house.

"I heard from some folks that you were hoping to move back to Maine and were thinking that maybe Carl would head there with you. Why do you think people are saying this, Missy?"

Her gaze turned quickly back to me, and her blue eyes seemed especially bright. Missy threw her head back and laughed.

"What is happening right now?" I asked her as she gathered herself.

Still smiling, she said, "Oh, Carr, if you could see your face. I'm sorry I startled you just now, but for real, I haven't laughed like that in, I can't tell you how long. This is really one of the funniest things I have heard in so long."

She wiped tears from her eyes and looked at me and decided to tell me more. "Carl is a real estate agent. I mean, Carl was a real estate agent. There would be no way he would have moved from here. Move to Maine? In the snow and cold, away from the Lowcountry? Absolutely no way, never. For heaven's sake, I don't know if I want to move back there, and I lived in the Northeast all my life! But us moving there together? That would never happen and it certainly would not happen because of me. And, by the way, I don't even know that I would have wanted that to happen. My divorce was just finalized a year ago, I'm not sure I even wanted a long-term thing with Carl, or with anyone right now."

She was gathering enthusiasm. "Carr, you do know he wasn't a real lighthouse keeper, right? You know he just lived in this house and occasionally worked in the museum? This lighthouse has a functional light, but all you have to do is flip a switch to turn it on. It's more of a courtesy than anything else. I mean, Carl could have never been a lighthouse keeper in a real, working lighthouse. You know this, right? So according to your source, I was going to bamboozle Carl into moving, away from an area he loved, to do a job he could never do? That's the story?"

She wasn't angry anymore. Missy seemed genuinely amused by this.

Talk about imposter syndrome. I felt completely ridiculous. Everything she said was something I logically knew, and yet, I had been swayed by the island gossip. It was the classic island rookie mistake and I fell for it. It was so maddening. I knew better than this. How many stories did we believe on our first trips to Mongin Island? We used to fall for all the "experts" who were so willing to share island tidbits with us, only for us to find out later those people often knew a small portion of the truth and built narratives around their own version of a story. What was I doing? I was running around, completely distracted. If I was going to help Julie, I needed to be better than this.

I met Missy's eyes directly. I was never one to shy away from a difficult conversation. To some, this meant I had an edge, but I always thought it was just much more efficient to speak plainly.

I told Missy, "When you put it that way, it does sound silly, doesn't it? You don't owe me an explanation. I know you don't. But we both want the same things, right? We both want to know what happened to Carl and if someone did something to him, we want to know who it was, do you agree?"

"Of course, yes. I want to know those things but I guess I didn't think of myself as any kind of suspect until I heard your word-on-the-street nonsense. Honestly, I did not know he was missing until I saw you. I am ashamed to say that I was so angry with him for the way we broke up and how fast he moved on, I just worked myself up with that story, that he was with Theresa. At the time, that made sense but now, looking at it, it sounds kind of stupid, saying it out loud. It was just too soon after my divorce to be cast aside again. God, that's so shameful and selfish."

She leaned forward. "Listen, Carr," she said, "I know you're trying to help Deputy Julie. Would it help you to see the inside of Carl's house? I still have a spare key. I locked it up after the detectives went through it. You never know if people will stop by if they think the house is empty. Morbid curiosity."

"Or if some people will just wander right in, right?" I tried to lighten the mood.

"Hmm, I heard that can happen." She smiled and went into her house to get the key.

Chapter 12

We walked together to Carl's house and were quickly inside. I noticed some of the paperwork that previously was on the table was missing, but overall things looked about the same.

Missy seemed to have her own list of concerns. "I want to ask Julie what I should do with the food in the refrigerator and the perishable things. I think we are good for another week or so, but I want to get rid of stuff before it starts rotting."

I walked into Carl's office. "What is the story with the map in here?"

"It's Mongin Island."

"Yes, but what are these pins?" The map was huge. It hung above several barrister bookshelves that lined the short wall of this office and was almost as wide as it was long. Many pins were stuck in all different locations on the map. There were a variety of red and blue pins, but only one green one. "These pins must mean something. Do you know what is going on here?"

"I don't, sorry," she said. "I know Carl sometimes stood right here and stared at the map, and one time he told me that this was his 'legacy', but I assumed he meant Mongin Island in general. You know he has—or *had* made many people's dreams come true through the deals he made. And Carl loved the stories of how people found their dream home—or now had money they never had before. Carl loved a good story."

"It's probably what made him so good at sales. He could find the human part of the transaction," I replied, though I was distracted. "Wait, see this green pin? Isn't this Governor's Point?" I was too short to see that portion of the map clearly, so I carried over Carl's desk chair and stood on it to get an eye-level view. "Bingo! Yes, it is!"

"So, I wonder," I started thinking out loud. "I wonder if this is some kind of sales tracker? It's going to be hard to say because this is just a map. There aren't property lines, but I bet we can test a few of these with some landmarks. Okay Missy, can you jot down a few things? Look, there is a red pin next to the community farm on the right side, still on Old Port Passage Way. And there is a blue one next to the school on the left side, closest to the water. Here is another red one on Church Street, right across the street from the church."

Missy was writing. "Wait, the one across from the church—wasn't that where Mr. Marshall lived? Carl sold his house to the new family with the twin girls. I can't remember their names."

"Yes, that's right! The Lane family. I met them at the general store when I first moved here and saw them again at Books & Brew last week. The girls are as sweet as gumdrops and so cute! Just learning to read! So, Carl was the agent for Mr. Marshall?"

"Definitely. The house needed some work and there were some negotiations, things the Lanes were asking for but if I remember right, Mr. Marshall's son did not want to do. Eventually, it all got worked out and Carl told me Mr. Marshall was happy there would be a young family in his house. Carl definitely sold that property."

"So, let's say the red pins are for properties Carl sold, but the blue ones are what? Current listings or leads? I need Carl's listing report," I said. "But then, what does the green pin mean?" We found a couple of more properties to test our theory and I hopped down from the chair. I told Missy I would review everything and be back in touch soon. She promised to reach out if she thought of anything else that would help.

"Before I go, one more question: Do you know Evan Weisman?"

"The sustainability guy? No, I don't know him, but I know of him. Well, not even really that, I just know Carl mentioned him to someone, once on a call. That's all I know." I found myself trying to determine if this really was all she knew. I came to see Missy to get answers but was leaving with more questions.

"Please let me know if you think of anything else," I said as I got into my cart. "Thanks, Missy."

I decided to visit one or two of these landmarks from the map. At each stop, I could not spot any obvious signs of sales activity. No real estate signs, no lockboxes. I identified and wrote down a few potential addresses based on the nearby streets. Surely, the public database of property records would show me which ones had recently been sold. I also assumed that files stored on Carl's computer would help me understand his map a little better.

After that, I gave Tripp a call and offered to pick up lunch. "That would be amazing Carr, you won't believe how busy we have been. This is our best sales day yet!"

I swung by the Dirt Road Diner and picked up two cheeseburgers with jalapeno poppers. This food truck was open for breakfast and lunch only, tucked off the side of Old Port Passage Way. There were a few tables and a dozen or so white resin chairs scattered around. It was an island staple. You could smell the burgers from down the road. I pulled in right before they closed and the ladies quickly cooked up our order. Before long, I was on my way back to the store and unpacking our lunch.

"Look at this! Buddy, come here!" I showed him the dog cookies the ladies had surprised me with at the bottom of our lunch bag. I guess everyone knew I had informally adopted Buddy.

"Dirt Road Diner, yum! Thanks, Carr," Tripp said, smiling broadly.

"Tripp, it's me who should thank you. You have done so much for the store and me. I really appreciate all you do. This is such a small little thing, but I want you to know how grateful I am for you and your hard work."

"Gosh, Carr, you're going to make me blush," he laughed. "I enjoy being here and I am happy to help you and our customers. It's all good, Carr, but thank you for saying it." We were all quickly busy with our meal, including Buddy, who was munching on his cookies, lying on my feet underneath the table.

"I didn't realize how hungry I was," I told Tripp, looking down at my half-eaten burger. "I had a busy morning and afternoon so far, but it sounds like you were busy, too. Look, Tripp, I want to fill you in on what I have learned so far about Carl's case, but I also don't want to put you in the position of people asking you for information."

"Honestly Carr, I don't really want to know. I just want to know when it's over. If Deputy Julie or you or anyone needs my help, I will help you, but I would rather not know all the details. I knew Carl for years, but not well. We weren't friends exactly, but I knew him well enough to talk to him at the Crab Shack or the Distillery. It may sound silly, but I would rather not know all the skeletons. You know I had a lot of struggles in my life. My life before my wife, Eloise, well, was pretty unhappy, and you know to lose her and Michelle Lynn right after, well, these were such hard, hard things. I loved teaching, but the last few years were tough, too. I came to Mongin Island to get away from the hard things. Some people call it an escape, and I guess it is."

"Maybe that's why we get each other, Tripp. I am escaping, too. This island can heal heavy hearts," I said. "I understand what you're saying, and I respect it completely. I will not make you part of this. I promise, we will get our island back, too, the way Mongin Island should be. We definitely will." Saying this out loud made it real.

"If anyone can do that, it's you!" And I could tell Tripp was done with this emotionally dense conversation. "Look at what you have done already. You broke sales records! Oh, and I forgot, geez, hold on—" He headed to the register. "Bob Harkins from East-West Books called and asked you to call him back. He said he was responding to your email."

The return call to Bob Harkins went to voicemail. I spent a few minutes updating my notes from the visit to Missy's and then, with new energy, I got to work on the floor, unpacking the remaining boxes of inventory. In no time at all, thanks to Tripp's efforts, the shop was looking great, the shelves were stocked, the register was cashed out and we were done for the day. We parted ways and Buddy and I headed home.

I had barely parked before my cell phone rang. "Hey, I know you didn't invite me, but I am bringing you dinner tonight. I made some chili and I am on my way, you can't say no!" Barb said all at once without a breath. "See you in about ten minutes." With that, the line went dead. I hadn't even answered her.

As I was scooping Buddy's food into his bowl, there was a knock on my porch door and Barb was walking through it, carrying a Crockpot with its lid snapped in place. "You haven't said one word, but I know what today is and I don't want you to be alone tonight. So here I am, sorry, but you're stuck with me at least for a few hours." She set the pot on the counter. "I have chili and some crusty bread. And a bottle of pinot grigio, so buon appetito to us!"

"Thank you, Barb. This is an incredible kindness, thank you," I said as I felt my eyes starting to fill for the first time today. "I just wanted to get through today. The kids and I are planning a little something tonight and I stayed busy all day, so that helped. It is hard to believe that I haven't seen my husband in a year—to think about all that he has missed, and what has happened this year. We spent over thirty years together and to just not be there, to not hear him, to not be able to tell him about even these small things in my day—it's just so—I don't know what it is …"

"It's awful, is what it is. He would have loved that you opened the shop, I bet, and that you have a dog again. I remember how much he loved playing on the beach with your two fuzzy girls. Boy, those dogs loved the water! Remember how you used those long leads to keep them from swimming away? We all thought they would paddle their way to the mainland if they could! Sanibel would be swimming with her two big old Lab ears, bobbing on the surface like yellow floaties. Remember how cute that was?" We both laughed, remembering all the pure joy of just being happy and present at that moment.

"Today was a good day, even though it was a hard day," I said simply.

"Was it? I'm glad for you. What made it a good day?" Barb sat back in her chair to listen and I told her about all that happened, from the positive feedback from the tourism group, to the record sales at the store, to the information I got from my talk with Missy and, of course, Carl's map with Governor's Point highlighted.

"As much as I want to believe Missy—and what she says does make sense—it was weird to me that being back in Carl's house didn't seem to spark any emotion in her. I mean, she and I had a real moment of connection outside in her yard. We were both pretty open about what we were thinking and how we could have handled things differently. I could see that she let the emotion of being rejected, passed over by Carl, cloud her judgment. But, if you felt that strongly, would you then not care at all when you went back into his house? I mean, her biggest concern was cleaning out the food. And that seemed off base to me." I looked at Barb as she poured us each another glass of wine.

"I hear you. It is a little weird, I agree," Barb said. "So, one minute you are saying, you got all worked up because Carl moved on too quickly—and then the next minute you're saying you're concerned with the vegetables and fruit in the fridge? It does seem off, but what do we really know about Missy? Maybe she is just a little off, maybe this is just her way. Just because you or I wouldn't react this way doesn't make her a killer. You have to admit, all the theatrics at Carl's house Saturday were kind of a lot."

"Right," I said. "It just doesn't sit right with me. I guess I got thrown off by Helen's stories about Missy. And now I want to be sure I am not missing anything else. I think I am going to see what some of our other islanders know about Missy."

Barb was more interested in Carl's map, and as I told her about it, she leaned forward and pushed our bowls and plates to the side. "Did Julie mention this to you?" she interrupted.

"No, and it wasn't on the evidence list she shared with me, but I wonder if they took pictures of it while they were out there at his house. It seems like Julie thinks my biggest help will be in talking to people and getting word-of-mouth background, but I have a feeling this map is telling us something. Governor's Point was marked a different way than the others. I think I can do more to help."

"Of course you do!" Barb smiled at me. "You and your overachieving self. Grab your computer, and let's dig into some of these properties."

I cleared the table and brought my laptop from the bookshelf in the family room. We were able to research all of the properties Missy and I found on Carl's map that were located near island landmarks. Using the county property records database, we were able to see the registrations of new deeds. From what we could tell, the red pins were properties sold in the last few years. Information from some online real estate sites was also helpful. One of the blue pins seemed to be tied to a current listing, although I did not see a for-sale sign in the yard. Barb said she would take a ride by that property in the morning to see if there was a lockbox on the front porch or something indicating it may be for sale. However, the green pin remained a mystery. Why was the very spot where Carl died marked in this unique way?

As we worked together on the laptop, I said, "I still don't have access to Carl's computer information from Julie. And I don't see the email Julie said she would send along, which is surprising. Hopefully, she will send it tomorrow morning. I want to see if there is a listing report in there. Carl owned his brokerage and didn't have a partner, but his listing report would show us what he was working on."

"Governor's Point has been basically abandoned for years. In all the times I went there, I never saw anyone, not one single person," Barb said. "But then Carl, who had the listing years ago and sold some of the lots, is found dead there. I am no detective, but that is not a coincidence."

I looked at the clock. Hours had passed. I told Barb, "If we aren't careful, we may end up on the county payroll." We made our plan for tomorrow and I updated my notes.

After Barb left, I settled down for our family video call. Even though I hated that we were having this conversation about Rob in the past tense, I recognized it was a wonderful way to celebrate him. Meredith and Nicholas both had so many stories to share about "their favorite thing Dad did." Over the years, we had enjoyed improvised song lyrics and amusement park trips, roller coaster rides, and learning to ski, so many good stories. The kids even had funny memories about times we had to discipline them.

It reassured me that although they missed their dad, the kids were mentally in a good place. They were sad but they were moving through the grief process in a healthy way. In all the talks and time together over the last year, this was the best they both sounded. We were getting there as a family, wherever this "there" was. Aside from them seeing Buddy on camera for the first time, the best part of the call was the news that both of them were coming to Mongin Island for Memorial Day weekend.

"You made me so happy tonight, both of you," I said to them. "Your dad loved you both so much, I am so proud of you and the people you have become, the way you handled this year. I can't wait for us all to be together. I love you guys!"

"Aw, Mom," Meredith said, "I'm sorry you had to be alone tonight and that we couldn't be there, but I am so glad we did this. It felt good to talk about all our happy memories!"

"Let's do a cookout when we are together. I'll grill," Nicholas said. "Grilling burgers and dogs after going to the beach, that'll be awesome! We can take Buddy for a long walk and he can sniff all he wants."

Our plans were made. The knowledge that it wouldn't be too long before we would be under one roof wrapped me like a cozy sweater on a cool night. I smiled as I settled myself into bed. Today was a good day. I was blessed with my children, my friends, and the possibility of still living a life of purpose. With gratitude, I was able to sleep peacefully and did not allow my mind to wander to the unanswered questions of Governor's Point.

Chapter 13

"Buddy, my friend, I hope you slept well. We are going to have a busy day today! Ready?" His tail was wagging in a circle. He seemed ready. We were off.

Our first stop was the General Store. I needed a few things, and I wanted to be sure I was able to get one of Miss Lucy's pies for the book club. I walked in on the last bit of Miss Lucy's conversation with Hetty, who was behind the counter at the store.

"Carr, look at these cute mini-pies Miss Lucy baked!" Hetty greeted me. The ceiling fan was working hard today, trying to push the humidity out the door. Fortunately, the air was still filled with the sweet scent of fresh pies.

"These are works of art!" I answered "Miss Lucy, what smells so good?"

"Girl, you are smelling my newest pie, the first run. Introducing my caramel turtle pie with a fabulous shortbread crust. You girls, be honest after you try it! Tell me if I should add it to the rotation. It's a pretty heavy pie, so I made these small ones in case someone just wants a little taste. Lots of butter in this recipe, that's for sure. Can't have this and say you're dieting!"

We all admired the pies with the golden-brown roped crusts. "The problem with your pies is that no one can stop after just a taste!" I said. "I will take a large and a small pie please, Hetty. This way I can guarantee that Tripp, Barb, and I will all get a taste of this masterpiece!"

Hetty packaged them up, along with my other necessities, and put a dog cookie in the strings of the pie boxes. "Just a little treat for your passenger." Hetty looked out the window next to the register. Buddy was snoozing in the front seat of my cart.

"How is Buddy doing?" Hetty asked. "That pup looks great! I wondered if his heart broke a little with Carl and all." Miss Lucy went to the door to get a glimpse of Buddy.

"He is seriously the sweetest baby," I said. "It's like we have always been together. He is very low maintenance, really, although I am sure he misses Carl. Carl rescued him from a shelter. Rescued dogs always seem to have a certain gratitude for their freedom."

"Any updates on Carl?" Hetty asked, and suddenly it felt like everyone's ears tuned in to the front counter. There were only a handful of people in the small shop, but I knew anything I said would ripple quickly to a much larger audience.

I tried to answer without really answering. "Deputy Julie is working through the details. I know she has collected a lot of evidence and is talking to people trying to learn more about Carl's last few days. Her team is working hard."

"Well, I don't know about all that," Hetty said, shifting behind the counter. "Seems like we should know more by now. Helen said that she heard Theresa is coming to the island. Did you know that? Seems Julie wants to talk to her, here on the island. I bet she wants to show her the crime scene. I heard Chief Lancaster saw Theresa and Carl together and so did a few of the resort staff. We were at the Crab Shack last night and seems like everyone there had a Theresa and Carl sighting." Hetty studied the cuticles on her right hand while her left hand rested firmly on her hip. Clearly, she wanted to hear more from me.

"Hetty, what do you know about Theresa?" I asked. "Does she live on the mainland?"

"Yeah, she lives on the mainland. She's some big deal over there, lives in one of the communities behind a gate. You know the kind, right? The ones where the people are better than the rest of us, according to them?" She answered quickly and included an eye roll for good measure.

"So, she has done well, I guess," I said. "But done well doing what?"

"She's a flip-flopper, or whatever you call it," Hetty said, looking completely uninterested in the whole conversation, even though she was the one who had started it.

"A flip-flopper?"

Miss Lucy clarified, "She is a property flipper, right Hetty? I think that is how they met. Theresa was interested in buying some island properties and flipping them. Carl was always looking for his next deal. A match made in heaven."

"So, were they an actual couple or just business partners?" I asked.

"I think they were a couple," Miss Lucy said. "Well, according to everyone, they seemed like a real couple and Carl ditched Missy pretty quickly after connecting with Theresa, although from what I heard, they have known each other for some time."

Soon, I was back in my cart and heading to Books & Brew. I quickly set up for the book club even though I did not expect their arrival for a few more hours. I had a selection of dishes I bought from the island potter, Boyd, years ago and today was a good day to use them. With small seashells lining each plate's edge, they were favorites of mine. The tea would be brewed when the ladies arrived but for the time being, I was as ready as I could be. This gave me a chance to settle into the back room, update my notes, and call Julie. It had only been a few days, but they were long ones, made longer by this unexpected and undefined role I was now playing. I was still unsettled after I visited Missy's yesterday. If I was going to be helpful, really helpful, I needed answers.

Julie answered immediately. "I was just about to call you, Carr. The data vault login is coming your way. Funny enough, our IT guys said some of the files were encrypted, but we got them all opened. One of our guys had to work through the night but they are digging in now and thought it would be awesome if you could also see what you can find. Our forensic accountant will not be available to us for at least two more days."

"Well, I made some progress, too," I said. "But I want to ask you about Theresa and the map on Carl's wall. Before we get into this stuff, though, I need to ask you, first, about me. Please, I hope you don't take this the wrong way, but I am not sure what I am actually doing."

Julie said nothing so I continued, "You asked me to help you, to listen and have conversations but in talking to people, things are happening. I'm hearing things and I'm seeing things like Carl's map. Like Carl's files, I mean you sent them to me now, but what am I doing? I know I offered to help with the files and the analysis and this is kind of a thing for me. But this is a big 'something'. Should I be digging into this? I just want to understand my role. Am I off-base with this?"

Julie sighed before she answered. "No, I don't think you're off-base. The fact of the matter is I haven't been entirely truthful with you. Guess you're a better detective than you think, Carr."

"What do you mean? How have you not been truthful? I can't be part of something if I don't know the whole story."

I guess I had expected Julie to be angry or maybe disappointed because I realized I was holding my breath, waiting for her response. "Totally fair, Carr. You have a right to ask," Julie said. "So, the truth is that we are in a really bad spot. The sheriff's department is extremely short-staffed. It's the worst it has ever been. Money is tight and everyone is pushed to their limits. But the way I see it, there is also a chance for us to make a good case for more funding if we solve cases quickly and use resources efficiently."

"I don't understand that. What do you mean?"

"Some time ago, the decision was made that the sheriff handles Mongin Island and the other barrier islands. The police handle the mainland. That's why the sheriff's department is here, handling this case."

"That didn't surprise me," I said. "As long as I have been coming here, the sheriff has always been coming to the island."

"But here is the root of the problem. We haven't really solved a murder in a very long time. Yes, there have been deaths, of course. But no murder in the last few years, not since Sheriff Oxley was elected. We have to get this right. We do have some high-profile cases in our jurisdiction. There are at least four major crimes right now, in addition to all the usual things. County resources are prioritized there. That's not to say we can't get the help we need to solve this case—but it may not be as fast as we want or need it to be."

"I see where you're going," I said. "Solving this case proves your department's capability, and your need for resources. Is that what you're saying?"

"Bingo, that's it." I could almost see her settling back in her chair, satisfied that her student had understood her lesson.

"So, you're willing to let me help as much as I can," I said. "I'm getting this now. As long as I don't tamper with evidence or do something off the wall, I can basically investigate, too." I knew the past few days had felt heavier than just helping out, but now I was understanding why. She needed me, needed us to do more, and she needed this help now.

"Julie, I wish you had just told me what you needed. Since we are still learning about this case, the people involved and each other, personally, I wish you just told me," I continued.

"Seriously, your help with the research and the conversations—such great stuff," Julie said. "You have a good eye, you're smart, and people like you. You can build rapport quickly. I appreciate what you have done and what you seem to want to do. And, you're right, I know I should have been more upfront with you. Honestly, given the shock you had and all the stuff on your plate, I am not sure if you would have been in a good place to agree to help. For better or worse, you came to the decision yourself. But truth be told, I guess I hesitated to ask a question I knew I may not want the answer to."

There it was. I wasn't going to get an apology for her lack of transparency. To continue working together, I would have to accept her acknowledgment that she could have been more direct and not look for more from her.

Julie hadn't forced me to get involved. I wanted to—and she welcomed my help. Julie hadn't asked me to figure out Carl's property map, she hadn't asked me to do the financial analysis. I made these decisions. I wanted Mongin Island to be a haven—the magical place I discovered on that first ride through the resort gates. Of course, I would do my part. That decision, that acceptance, didn't erase my wish that she had been more upfront. Maybe that is unreasonable, given that just a few days ago Julie was a complete stranger. We didn't have this long relationship built on trust and respect. Maybe I was asking too much.

"Julie, I will help you solve the case. Not for your sake, but for Mongin Island's sake. But, from this point forward, let's be honest. As much as I want this behind us, it won't work for me to think that there is more to what you are telling me. Are we good?"

"Totally understand, you have my word," Julie said. "So, ready to talk about where we are? I spoke to Theresa yesterday. According to her, they were a real couple, have known each other for at least a year or two, but only started a romantic relationship in the last month or so. Her story seems to check out. She seemed appropriately sad about Carl's passing but she was not distraught. She was aware of potential motives for harm to have come to Carl and mentioned a few unfinished deals but did not have specifics. But, I do think she knows more than she's telling me."

"Why is that? Because they both were chasing deals? That's what I was thinking as you were talking."

"Exactly. It seems like this would be the thing that would draw you together, unless, of course, you didn't want to be drawn together in a deal. To me, this would seem counterintuitive. If you are just starting this new relationship after knowing each other for a few years, that doesn't sit right for me," Julie said. "So we are digging around on that, which leads me to the property map in the office."

Ahhh, the map. I wondered if she would mention it. "From what I can tell, red pins mark the properties Carl sold," I said. "There are lots of them, all over this island. Did you notice how many pins were red? Then, I think the blue ones are Carl's current listings and possibly properties with a lead, maybe something that would come to market soon or a work in progress. There weren't really as many of those, only a handful. I'm not sure how many, right now. I'll have to count them."

"There were eleven blue pins," Julie answered. So, now I knew this map was part of the investigation.

"Which leads me to the green pin at Governor's Point!" I finished a little more dramatically than I intended. "Something is up there. If it was just a regular listing, it would be blue, right? So, something is going on there and I thought I would reach out to the developer, if that is okay with you. I want to understand the Governor's Point project. Barb and I were doing some research last night. Looks like there are fourteen lots in that subdivision and three appear to have been purchased. It also makes sense to talk to those property owners."

"Sounds good," Julie said.

"Also, Missy was vaguely aware of the name Evan Weisman. She said he was in some sustainability business, which is a tip I will explore as I dig into Carl's files."

"That could narrow down the right Evan Weisman—so that's great info. We will explore it on our end, too. Scott Campino is the Governor's Point developer and he lives there on the island. Do you know him?" Julie asked, "I have a cell number for him. I'll text it to you."

"I haven't met Scott," I said. "I do know Donna Campino, who may be his wife. Before I moved here full-time, we socialized with our neighbors and some people we met playing golf. We didn't know too many island residents. Of course, with the store, I meet a lot more people now. Donna has been in the store a few times and donated some books to the Trading Floor. Seems like a nice lady."

"Do you think you can get to Scott today?" asked Julie. "He may be able to connect you to the property owners too."

"I certainly can try," I agreed. "I have about ninety minutes before the shop opens and usually, we aren't that busy when the doors first open. I can spend some time on Carl's computer files, too. But what about Theresa? Are you interviewing her in person, here on the island?"

"Well, not exactly interviewing her," Julie said. "Let's just say we invited her to take a ride over on the 2:00 ferry and hoped she would show us some of the properties she and Carl looked at for potential flips. She accepted our invite, thankfully. We are meeting her at the dock at 2:45. If that works for you, I would love to have you join us. Now that you have spoken to Missy a few times, talking to Theresa may help us get to know Carl a little better."

"You can count on me being there," I said. "I'm curious about Theresa myself. See you soon, Julie, and thanks for getting this all out and clearing the air. I think we are on the right path now."

The shop was quiet. There was a stillness inside and outside the building. I grabbed my laptop and sat on the front porch, settling into one of the new rockers. I could check my email from here and start the work I had in front of me. The gentle rocking was soothing. The rhythm pulsed my thoughts, my unspoken words, away.

It didn't take long to go through the dozen or so new messages in my inbox. "Okay, so I have two nibbles on my inquiries about Paul's rare books. Hmm, better than I expected," I told the squirrel precariously balancing on the porch railing.

Chapter 14

Of the two replies, Monica Parker's email was particularly interesting. Among my new book contacts, she represented a group of mainly nonfiction publishers who hired her to represent books that I was not likely to find in *Publishers Weekly* or other book lists that were coming my way these days. I liked her entrepreneurial spirit in working with smaller publishing houses and I was not surprised that she responded so quickly to my email. I dialed the cell number listed in her signature block and she answered on the second ring.

"Hey, Monica!" I said when I heard her answer.

She went right to business. "So, Carr, what exactly are you up to in that little shop?"

"Monica, you can't imagine. I never expected to deal in rare and antique books, but that was one of my first requests from a customer. Who knows? Maybe that's a good option for me, since I'm running a bookstore on a historic island." We discussed Paul, his historical knowledge, past efforts to find these books, and the urgency of his request.

"Well, to be honest, this is going to be tough—and expensive," Monica said. "To start with, you knew these books were out of print and have been for—well, it looks like for two centuries in one case!

They're not on any library inter-loan list, so that's not a solution. Then, because it's not in the library systems, Google Books never scanned these. And I'm sure you or your customer checked the obvious online auction sites. I know that I did. Nothing there. Now, that doesn't mean we can't get them, but let's be honest, these were short runs by small publishers that just don't exist anymore. That's a much trickier request, for all the reasons you can imagine."

She continued, "I do have some good news for you. I have a lead on one of the rarest volumes your customer requested. *The Story of the Carolinas, Vol. XXXVI of The Modern Part of an Universal History,* leather bound and published in London in—what's MDCCLXXV?"

"1775," I said. "And I'm starting to get the picture that this is going to be a tough request to fulfill, right?"

"Right," Monica said. "And I won't even try to read the full slate of names that are listed as publishers. But the title page says, 'Printed for S. Richardson, T. Osborne, C. Hitch' and then there are about a dozen other names 'and the Polymath Club.'"

"I'm impressed!" I said. "You got right to it!"

"Okay, well at least I've got a line on one of these books for your client. And—let me look at this email again as I'm talking to you." There was a pause. I heard the clicks. "Right. yes, that's the correct book and it only showed up because there was a Washington D.C. newspaper clipping that turned up in one of my friend's searches that mentions this guy who's an Atlantic shoreline historian. My friend followed that *Post* clip back to this historian's website and, as it turns out, he wrote a blog post some years ago about this series of books in his library. He's got a photo of the title page of *The Carolinas* volume and a little back story about how these books survived various disasters over the years. There are actually a few little holes in one corner of the page in the photo he posted, because sometime in the last couple hundred years, someone who owned it had an infestation of bookworms! They didn't destroy the books, and they're long, long gone, but they nibbled a little on the corners. Let's say your *Carolinas* book is very appropriately distressed for an eighteenth-century volume."

"I'm in awe," I said. "You guys did this so fast. So, did you make contact with this historian? Should I make contact? Do you think he'd sell the book?"

"I have no idea yet," Monica said. "And, no, don't try to reach him directly. My friend and I are pursuing this. I will have more information, probably in a day or two, but I wanted to ask you before we go much further on this: How much is this guy willing to pay? I need to know what I am working with before we reach out."

"I think my client will be willing to pay. Seems like he's got money, you know. He specifically told me I would be rewarded for finding these books, so I assume he understands that we all expect fees here, plus the cost of the book. It didn't seem that there were financial limits, but I will check. What else do I need to know?"

Monica said, "I say that you should make your phone call to him, and I will make my calls. I still have a few ideas to pursue on the other volumes, but I am heading in a good direction with probably the rarest on his list. Let's touch base after you talk to your client. For now, I have what I need."

Then, before I picked up the phone to call Paul, I turned to the second email—the one from Bob Harkins of East-West Books.

"Carr, great to connect," Bob said when I reached him.

"Thanks for your email," I said.

"Sorry we missed each other when I stopped by the island the other week," he said. "I was in the region for a writers' conference at Savannah-Mercer for a couple of days. So, it was an impulse thing to hop on a ferry to see your Mongin. Your descriptions—plus the books and movies about the island—make that place seem like another world, another time. I thought I'd soak up a few hours of the local color and surprise you. I did leave a box for you with Tripp. I wish now that I had called in advance. We could have had lunch in Savannah."

"I was surprised when I heard you rode the ferry over," I said. "Sorry I missed you. I was hot on the trail of my new cash register— or, I should say, my new old cash register. I wanted an antique and ended up finding a good one. It's a little clunky but most people have patience for the slow pace."

"Sounds like things are going well at the store. But I have to say, I was more than a little surprised you're already digging into antiquarian searches."

"This has all happened so fast, I never even thought about rare books but this request came from a customer. We are starting to pick up some steam and I want to build a loyal customer base. And this customer, in particular, doesn't seem like he is used to hearing 'no' often. I tried every which way to set reasonable expectations. He is a regular visitor to the island, so this could be a long-term relationship."

"Fascinating. Your island is full of mystery, and your customer has some well-developed requests, that's for sure. Tough for you to start with these—these are some heavy hitters."

I was eager to encourage Bob, so I added, "I've still got your latest email about the summer titles you're representing. I'll be ordering soon. I am really starting to understand the demographics here."

"Excellent!" he said. "And I have a new author from Florida who I want to showcase in your part of the country this summer. He's retired and well off and he's paying his own way on an Atlantic Coast book tour—and he hired me to help with the logistics. He and his wife want to explore all the places they said they would travel to someday. I think he'd be ideal for a day on Mongin. He is interested in the regional history, has seen some of the movies shot on the island, I think you would enjoy meeting him. His book is in that box I left."

"Book tour! How exciting—I think residents and tourists would like an event like this. I would love to offer it at the shop, so send me some more details on this author and we'll talk. I like this idea."

"Right," he said. "Then, let's get to today's business. Today we're talking about these antiquarian requests. This is some list, Carr. Not exactly beach reads, that's for sure. What's the story here?"

We covered Paul's thirst for this material, and I tried to convey his urgency for a resolution to a problem on which he would not elaborate. I told Bob that Paul isn't a full-time resident and seemed eager to finish some research before leaving again in a matter of weeks.

Bob asked the question that also puzzled me, "What's he studying?!"
"That I don't know," I answered. "He's a bit of a riddle, to be honest."
"Is he a journalist trying to break a 200-year-old story?"
I laughed. "No, he's not a journalist, at least as far as I know. So far,
I'm chalking this up to 'Island Mysteries.' I've been coming to Mongin
for more than a decade, but in these months since I've settled in as a
resident, I keep meeting people with—well, with mysteries swirling
around them."

Bob said, "Well, I'm happy to help. I have to branch out. You know,
book agents like me are an endangered species these days. People are
buying more books every year than ever before, but the Big Five have
squeezed the margins so close that those golden advances that used
to be our bread and butter are long gone. Unless you've got celebrity
clients—and I haven't managed to land a movie star or a former pres-
ident yet. If you're not a heavy hitter, there's very little money up front,
if any at all. There's certainly no more money for publisher-paid book
tours. So, my expansion into other fields is what's keeping me afloat.
I've now signed a half dozen authors to independently rep their
launches. And that, Carr, is a very long way of admitting to you that
I'm not exactly an expert in the antiquarian market. However, I am
taking on some rare book inquiries to shore up the bottom line."

"I understand and I appreciate that. Seems like change is certainly
inevitable in all industries these days. So, tell me more, I certainly
appreciated your email."

"Of course," he said. "I wrote right away because I do think I have
a lead on one book, but it's from a private collector. Everything about
this tells me this is going to be expensive, very expensive. From what I
hear, this collector can trace a direct family lineage to the early 1700s
in your region of the country. If he is willing to part with this book, it
will be very expensive."

"Sounds like that might be the case," I agreed. "I am curious about
this collector. What else can you tell me?"

"Not much, sadly. Collectors often want to stay in the background.
So, this will be my part of the mystery."

"My customer did make it clear he expects to pay reasonable fees to get these books. To ballpark, would you guess we are talking hundreds, or maybe thousands? What do you think?"

Bob took a deep breath and said, "I admit that this is out of my wheelhouse, but a former colleague of mine in New York now is very active in this market. When I got your list, I called him with it. He's the one who found this source and agreed to keep me in the deal. So, I will be honest with you. I actually don't have too many more details to share at this point. What I can tell you is that my friend now deals in famous first editions—you know, books that go up for auction through Christie's and the like for six figures. He's doing me a favor here, because we've known each other for years, but I get the sense from him that this will run into the thousands easily, maybe tens of thousands. And, at this point, he doesn't even know if his source is willing to sell, so that puts more pressure on the deal. I wanted to find out how serious your guy is about this before I ask my friend to go further."

As I had with Monica, Bob and I confirmed the title and edition. As he read me the listing of names from the Polymath Club, I got a chill and my stomach turned a little. "What are you reading from, Bob?"

"My friend sent me a photo."

Instantly, I suspected Bob and Monica might be closing in on the same collector, and I debated whether I should say anything more. I certainly did not want to touch off a bidding war. I took a breath and was just about to tell Bob about Monica when I hesitated. Did I really know enough to suspect they might have the same collector in mind? I didn't know their sources. They might be entirely different collectors. I intentionally asked nothing more about this photograph, but knew I did not have long to figure this out.

"Ummm, Bob, let's do this," I said. "I'll call my customer and find out more about his budget. On your end, please get back to me as soon as you know more about this collector. I'd like to know more details before your friend starts any negotiations."

"Makes sense," he said. "Maybe we all can make a few dollars, make your customer happy and start a whole new line for Books & Brew."

"Let's hope," I said, still a little anxious about not telling Bob more. There were just so many things to process in the last few days, I really did not feel sure of much right now.

All of this would have to wait. I needed to get to Paul. I hit his contact on my phone and waited for him to answer. Just before my call went to voicemail, he picked up and I was greeted with his immediate annoyance.

"Yes, Carr," he said brusquely. "What news are you bearing today?"

I quickly went through the updates Bob and Monica had shared, careful not to share too many details. Everyone in this deal was protecting valuable information—and so was I. Then, I outlined the potential cost, going with Bob's estimate and not mentioning that Monica had not yet ballparked a price. I needed to test the high end to weigh Paul's commitment.

"So, what if we come back with an offer that's more than ten thousand dollars?" I asked.

Paul was silent. I wondered if our call had dropped. "Hello? Paul? You still there?"

"I am contemplating," he said. "Frankly, I had hoped, well, at the risk of sounding mildly ungrateful, I had hoped your contacts would have performed better for you—for us. I had hoped that someone might have been able to locally source options for me. These seem like books that might have been retained by older families. I was envisioning dusty leather-backed volumes just taking up space on someone's parlor shelves, you know—someone who might feel honored that a researcher wanted to obtain one of their volumes. I was envisioning a contact I might be able to pursue and pick up these books for a matter of—" Then, he fell silent again. Finally, he said, "Oh, perhaps a few thousand dollars overall. Something that would be an easy transaction, something that flies under the radar."

This was equally disappointing and illuminating. He wanted a deal that would not bring undue attention. I had not told him much about Monica or Bob and now I was glad I had not. Monica worked out of Chicago and Bob's office was in Philadelphia. Paul seemed to have assumed that I somehow had book contacts in coastal historical societies. At the moment, I had two legitimate leads toward finding Paul's rarest book and several people—including myself—already had spent hours on his search. Could he find a copy for a few thousand dollars? It didn't seem likely. Part of me wanted to question him. Afterall, he made it sound that money was no object and that I would be rewarded for my efforts. Yet, now with an active lead, was he hesitating? After years of searching? This reaction was disorienting.

Paul had fallen silent again.

I made my point by switching to the past tense. "Paul, we did the best we could. These are extremely rare books. My contacts and I searched all the usual databases. We collectively asked experienced professionals to help, using their networks. If your budget is limited, I can contact them and close out this matter."

This guy was draining. He was smart and clearly was experienced in historical research. He must understand something about this market.

"Frankly, I am running out of time," he said finally. "Time, unfortunately, is not on my side in this process. So, I believe I may have no choice. This Plan B you have outlined for me is very unappealing. At my bidding, you have started inquiries and have kindly pointed out that the antiquarian market is indeed the correct avenue for this procurement. The fact that no one could find these through the usual searches does not surprise me. You can be assured, I have exhausted those options myself. I do thank you for this sliver of hope and I am willing to proceed."

"Okay Paul, I will communicate this to my contacts, that you are willing to move forward," I said. "That is, if the budget works for you." I thought he would have jumped at the idea of finally having the text he wanted after all these years of searching. At this point, I almost felt like I was convincing him. His wavering was unexpected. What was really going on with him?

"Please proceed," he finally said. "However, when you are closing in on a specific offer, I will want the seller to send me proof in the form of some photographs."

"Of course," I said. "And, depending on the price, there should be an examination of the book at the time of sale. At more than ten thousand, an in-person examination is a given."

He did not respond to that. He apparently was still focused on his own line of thinking. "Photographs will be a requirement in the process, before any check is cut or meeting is set. Photographs of some specific pages I will send to you and you can convey to the seller," he said.

"Okay, then," I said. "Photos would be a reasonable step. I will make sure I outline your request."

As the call ended, I realized I was shaking my head.

"Didn't go as you thought?" Tripp asked over my shoulder.

"No, but I can't figure out why."

"Maybe you are just seeing mysteries everywhere." Tripp tried to sound encouraging, but I still felt like I was missing something.

With Paul's direction outlined, I fired up my email once again and began writing very carefully worded emails to Monica and Bob. But now I knew to anticipate more mysterious twists from Paul. Photographs of some specific pages? Then, it clicked! Why hadn't I seen this the moment he mentioned photos? If he got his photographs, would Paul balk at the final sale of the entire book itself? What exactly did Paul want? A book or information from the book? Clearly, I would have to negotiate more carefully myself and limit what pages we would request.

Soon enough, I would have to address the question regarding Bob and Monica's sourcing, as it was weighing heavily on me. Life had taught me that if things like this keep themselves in the foreground, it is likely best to tackle head on and soon. I needed to pause on this until my head was a little clearer and I could find the right words.

For now, I put Paul and his demands out of my mind. It was time to learn a little more about Carl. I was eager to use the login Julie had sent me.

The data vault holding Carl's files was organized by file type. There were so many spreadsheets, so they seemed to demand my attention first. I flagged a couple for further review but the one that caught my eye was the export from Carl's bookkeeping software. It was a year-to-date record of his business revenue and expenses—and it was impressive. Carl ran his business well. Expenses were low. Without an office and having a small geographic territory on which to focus, it seemed he managed his costs very well. Marketing was Carl's biggest investment, which was completely reasonable when you factor in all the ads, photography, and printed material in real estate marketing. Carl had expensed a few meals and gifts for clients but there was nothing concerning or unusual in his records.

On the revenue side, his reputation seemed well-founded. Carl collected commission from sales and rentals monthly and there were many months with multiple transactions. Carl's real estate business was healthy and impressive. Other spreadsheet tabs showed the history from prior years. Overall, it was quite remarkable. As Helen had said, he had done very well. We would need to spend time confirming the accuracy of this information, but at first glance, it looked solid. Carl kept detailed records, was a conscientious business manager and, by all accounts, a solid real estate broker.

Opening Carl's database of listings was a gold mine. Each property's description included the homeowner's information, activity, showings, and links to the plat and information on file with the county. The dashboard on the home page made it easy to run reports and with three clicks, I had Carl's current listing report sent to the printer across the room. As expected, the blue pin properties were there. Noticeably absent were any Governor's Point lots, requiring me to dig deeper. Nothing I found so far explained the green pin.

Sifting through Carl's historical activity, I found the three Governor's Point lots he sold years ago. Interestingly, the buyers for these lots were the same people as those currently listed on the county property records. I found myself saying out loud: "I wonder if these people are holding on to these things, waiting for something good to happen, or if they just can't get rid of them?"

I needed to talk to someone who might be able to get me a lead on this mystery, so I began preparing a list of questions for Scott Campino. This was going to be challenging. Should I think of Scott as a source of helpful information, a suspect, or both? But that call would have to wait.

Thirty minutes before the store opened, I turned on the lights, started the ceiling fans, brewed some fresh tea for the carafes, and prepped the store. As I raced around with the floorboards creaking beneath me, I rehearsed the conversation I anticipated having with Scott, trying to navigate my questions about the murder scene and to find some clue to the mysterious green pin. I began to test the sound of my planned questions.

"No, not in years!" Tripp's booming voice jolted me back to reality.

"Tripp, you scared me half to death. How long have you been in here? Seriously, I just jumped a mile!"

"Sorry Carr, I heard you talking and I just assumed you were talking to me. I said 'Good morning', and you asked me if I had been to Governor's Point lately." He looked just as confused as I had felt.

"I was rehearsing what I am about to say to Scott Campino. Sorry, Tripp, I didn't realize I was speaking out loud." I sheepishly looked at him. "I thought you were coming in at noon? Sorry for the goofy start to the day!"

I headed right to the office, mission-focused and ready. One quick sip of my peppermint tea later, Scott Campino's phone was ringing.

Chapter 15

Was it a good sign that he answered on the third ring, just as I thought the call would go to voicemail? After a few minutes of introductions and chit-chat about Books & Brew, I shifted gears and told him why I hoped we could spend a few minutes talking about Governor's Point. Scott seemed to be aware that I was helping Julie. She already had talked to him, but he was willing to answer my questions as well.

"Until last Saturday," I said, "I had never been to Governor's Point, even in all the years of coming to the island. Why don't we start at the beginning with your plan and all that. It really is a beautiful piece of property."

"Sure, just stop me if you need me to fill in any of the blanks here." Scott seemed unguarded and began an introduction to Governor's Point that sounded like he had presented it many times before. His story started with finding the property, purchasing it in an off-market deal, and then dividing the big land parcel into fourteen lots. He explained he decided to size the lots at about one acre to ensure landowners had some privacy. Carl facilitated the deal from a private buyer, because somehow Carl knew the former owner could be convinced to sell.

"Carl always had his finger on the pulse of this community," Scott said. "He just *knew* this island. He knew about potential sales, even if the buyer or seller didn't live on the island. He had this sixth sense, I guess you could call it. He knew every inch of this island, I swear. He could see a potential deal where no one else could."

"So, this deal was your first with Carl?" I asked.

"I didn't really know Carl that well, all those years ago, but I had built a few houses here and a few on the mainland. He approached me about Governor's Point and honestly it was a little bigger than I thought I could or even should take on at that time. My father-in-law loaned me the money to buy the land and I went for it."

"And you put up the money for the improvements?"

"Well, the dock was already established, but it was my wife's idea to build the pool and the clubhouse to help people envision living in this neighborhood. After that was built, we managed the pool and the yard work ourselves. It was easy to swing by and just spend an hour or so there. Our kids loved it too. They could go for a quick swim while we did a few things around the property."

Three lots sold quickly, Scott explained. For a while, he had showings, then the economy turned and interest in the property dried up. Even the early landowners were afraid to move forward without momentum. "We were just circling the drain, really. I felt pretty good about the fact I could pay back my family, but we lost money on the pool and clubhouse. The Inn and all the resort-property construction hurt Governor's Point. You know, the downturn in the economy, in general, didn't really help us either. It's expensive to build on an island and I get it, most people don't want to invest a lot of money in a property that looks like what Governor's Point looks like right now. We needed a special kind of buyer, but that's a small demographic, which is why I was pretty surprised Carl called me, one day about a month ago."

"And?" I prompted.

I was holding my breath. "For many years, I focused on building on the resort and in several of the other neighborhoods. People, you know how it is, a lot of people know your business better than you, according to them, well, people would say I was working against myself by building things that would compete against my own property. But I could not afford to build on spec, I was building in other places for actual customers."

Scott went on, "Things were busy and I always intended to get back to Governor's Point, but really, I had a lot of work and it just stayed on my list of something I would focus on after this or after that, it just never happened. Taxes are low, carrying costs are low, I guess it was easy to put it on the shelf. So when Carl called, I was surprised."

"He told you there was interest in Governor's Point?" I asked.

"It had been several months since we last spoke," Scott said. "Then, out of the blue he called and said he had recently been introduced to a man who was looking for a piece of land, about fifteen acres or so. This guy wanted to develop the land in an environmentally responsible way and Carl asked if I would talk to him. Man, I jumped at the chance!"

There were so many things I wanted to ask and Scott was very willing to share all he knew. Our conversation just flowed. Before we finished, Scott had provided a complete picture of his history with Governor's Point, but not the identity of this potential buyer who Carl had never named. Scott and Carl last spoke on Thursday morning and were supposed to meet on Saturday afternoon to walk the property. After Carl was found at Governor's Point, Scott wondered if all of his hopes for this land were forever in the past.

"So Carl did not mention someone named Evan Weisman to you?"

"Evan Weisman, the Newport developer? Heck no. Is that the buyer's name? He is a huge real estate investor, too."

"To be honest, Scott, I am not really sure. His name has been tossed around as someone Carl had been spending time with recently. He is an investor with an interest in environmentally friendly development, so I wondered if this was your mystery man."

"I mean, that would have been out of this world. He has been growing his portfolio and is all over the trade magazines, but I don't know him personally. Carl did tell me I might have to sign an NDA before the meeting I was supposed to have on Saturday. Maybe it was Mr. Weisman, I really don't know."

I thanked Scott—sincerely. "It was really great to talk to you, Scott, appreciate all your insight here. I took good notes, but we may have some follow-up. Is it okay with you if I reach out again?" Talking to Scott was like talking to someone I had known for years.

"Call me any time, Carr, and I want to come meet you in person. Donna has raved about your store and I told her I'm fixin' to sit on your porch with one of my crime books. One day soon, I am going to do just that," he said warmly.

We hung up.

"Let the day begin!" I announced to Tripp and Buddy, feeling the energy of progress. Customers already were sitting on the porch and several were exploring the featured-author shelves. Maybe I would add the Florida author to this display, especially now that tourists were arriving.

Chapter 16

The Trading Floor was ready for Helen's book club and in short order, the ladies arrived. They were a mismatched group. Helen was clearly in charge, assigning seats and swapping chairs. Sally Ann's arms were filled with her baby daughter tucked into her infant carrier, a white cozy receiving blanket, and three books. Joyce's silver hair framed her face and if you looked closely, you could see her bright red glasses nestled among it. She used her cane to make room for Sally Ann, pushing a chair closer to the doorway, inviting her to sit there.

Julia quietly found her seat, smiled serenely at the group, and said, "It is so wonderful to be here with all of you. And thank you, Carr, for hosting us." I could tell she was a noticer. As they sat around the long table, their collective excitement filled the room.

"I am thrilled to do this!" I said. "In honor of your first meeting here, we brewed some tea and I have one of Miss Lucy's specialties. Just let me know when you are ready or if you need anything. For now, I will leave you to it!" I turned to head back to the main room.

Helen appeared at the register after some time and I knew they were ready for refreshments. "This pie looks amazing, I can't wait for you to try it," I said as I was loading up the tray with plates, napkins, and forks.

"It does look incredible," Helen said. "Before we go back in, I wanted to ask you if there was any news. Any updates you can share? Did you poke around with Missy? Something is not right there, I know it, and what about Theresa? She is coming here today, is she in danger?"

From the other room, Joyce shouted, "Helen, bring Carr over near us so we can all hear!"

As we served the tea and pie, the ladies bounced their theories off each other like Ping Pong balls. For each idea tossed into the discussion, one of them would debunk it and the next possibility would be served up almost immediately. My head was spinning. Then, the first taste of pie quieted the group and I saw my opportunity to change the subject.

"Tell me what you know about Paul Easton," I said.

"Who?" Sally Ann asked, "Who is that?"

"Bless your heart, Carr! You poor baby! Has Paul made an appearance here? I knew he had arrived for his yearly visit but I heard he has been all caught up with his special project. Has he been fussing at you?" Helen protectively placed her hand over mine.

"No, not really," I said. "Actually, he needs some books and I am trying to help him find them. He is on some kind of a deadline so we are trying to move quickly."

"I still don't know who Paul Easton is," Sally Ann said.

After Joyce filled her in, Julia said, "Several years ago, Paul said something that has stayed with me. I found it so profound that it just stayed with me. Every year, I say I am going to ask him when I see him next, and then when that opportunity comes, he is so intimidating, I just think it would sound ridiculous to bring up a passing comment he made years ago."

"Well, are you going to tell us what he said?" Helen said.

Julia smiled, sipped her tea and said, "Helen, I doubt you will feel the same way about it. When was the last time we agreed on the nuances of a particular line from our readings? You and I see things differently, which is what keeps our book club so interesting, right?"

"And—" Helen was impatient. "And he said—"

Clearly, Julia had achieved her desired effect. She sipped her tea again before she said, "Paul told me he has a history here on Mongin Island that is older than our country, deeper than any grave we can find here, spanning international boundaries."

No one said anything for a moment.

"That's your idea of a passing comment?" Joyce said.

Helen asked, "What on earth could that mean?"

I said, "I am not sure what he means, but that's one thing I intend to find out." Paul being forthcoming with this information was just as curious as the statement itself.

The group's reading selection still had some areas to be explored and Joyce, this session's appointed discussion leader, had outlined a few more exploratory questions, so I excused myself and stepped outside to clear my head.

It was another phenomenal day on Mongin Island: blue sky, puffy white clouds, the faint smell of suntan lotion, and salt air hinting at the day's possibility. From the porch's side, I could see several old oaks, dripping in Spanish moss. It was all so familiar and comforting. Standing on this deck, even for these few minutes, allowed me to refocus. Layers of Carl's story were added today. He was a successful businessman who seemed to act ethically. He also was a neighbor, a community member, a boyfriend, and a friend. Likely, there was a thread, tying him to someone already on our radar, that somehow broke. I needed to find that thread.

Refreshed, I returned to the store's main room. My eyes went to Buddy, curled up once again with Jacob.

"Well, hello, Jacob. How's your day going?"

"Hi Miss Carr, my day is great! I love my new school, but today we got out early because the teachers have to go to a class. On regular days, we get to play outside every day and have time before and after school to read. I have three new friends and I am going to a birthday party this weekend!" His whole face lit up as the words tumbled out. I loved watching the fingers on his left hand softly twirl Buddy's ears while he held a book in his right hand. Both of his legs tapped the base of his club chair. All this energy in one little body!

"Wow, Jacob, that makes me so happy. Three new friends—you are a lucky guy, that's for sure. And reading time, too! I like your new school. What are you up to today?"

"I'm looking for a book on seashells. My mom and I have been collecting things from our walks. There are so many cool shells here!"

As I sat down next to him, he filled me in on some of the different treasures he found on their beach walks. He found a starfish the other day. His eyes were wide with the joy of telling someone about something that he really liked to do.

"Did you ask Mr. Tripp about any shell books in the Trading Floor? Mr. Tripp knows everything that is in there. I swear, he doesn't miss a trick!"

As if on cue, Tripp appeared. "Hey, Jacob, have you ever considered using a metal detector on your beach walks? My neighbor has one and I would be happy to introduce you and your mom to him. He is always looking for people to share a walk with him and he has a few grandchildren that visit regularly. Should I mention this to your mom?"

I heard them discuss how a metal detector works as they walked together to the next room. Tripp had years of practice explaining things to children. Jacob's excitement bounced off our walls. His confidence to ask questions and his enthusiasm to try something new were so heartwarming to witness. He was growing, right before our eyes.

"Okay with you if I walk him back to the resort? I can't wrap my head around him wandering out alone." Tripp popped his head back into the room, looking for his sunglasses.

"Of course! Buddy wouldn't mind a jaunt with you guys, if you want some company." They were off and I got started on planning the rest of my day. When he returned, Tripp joined me in the back room and teased, "Who knew we were such softies?" We smiled at each other and I said, "It's true, any time I see a child reading, it melts my heart. There is a kindness, a goodness to that child and I want him to know we see him, just the way he is."

We decided Tripp was going to work on our website, and he had some ideas for the events page. "At the rate you're going, we are going to have a lot of updates to that page!" he said. "Are you going to meet Deputy Julie now?"

"I am, if you're good with keeping Buddy here. I will head out and should be back before closing," I replied. A minute or two later, I was on my way to the Mongin Island landing. This trip only took a few minutes but by the time I arrived I had dozens of questions I really wanted—I really needed—to ask.

Chapter 17

The sheriff's boat had already brought Deputy Julie and Lieutenant Cole over from the mainland and they had their black Tahoe pulled up to the gangway, right next to the front parking lot. On an island full of golf carts, this scene drew many curious looks from the passengers waiting to board the next ferry. As I approached, Julie climbed out of the car and we walked together to meet the incoming ferry. The water lapped against the wood pylons. The smaller boats, tied to nearby slips, bobbed in the gentle waves. We walked in silence. The easy camaraderie we previously shared definitely felt strained, at least to me.

"There it is now, pulling around the cove," Julie said as she shaded her eyes with her right hand. "I've heard quite a few things about Theresa. I wonder what will end up being true."

"I actually have the opposite problem," I answered. "So far, no one can really tell me much about Theresa, except that she was dating Carl, lived in a gated community, and was active in the real estate market. I feel like there are a lot of things to explore, that's for sure."

As the passengers disembarked, we spotted Theresa immediately, walking confidently toward us. Her outstretched hand was perfectly manicured and complemented by a large silver and gold ring twisted into a knot. She wore coral-colored pants, a crisp white top, and designer wedge sandals. It was her necklace that immediately caught my eye: a Van Cleef and Arpels vintage clover necklace. My mother was gifted a similar one years ago and it was now among my most treasured possessions.

After brief introductions, Julie shepherded us back to the Tahoe. Theresa and I climbed into the back seats. If Theresa was curious about my role, she did not reveal it. Her face was unreadable. Once the doors were closed, Julie asked a few questions that Theresa answered simply. She confirmed she and Carl had known each other for almost two years—and had worked on some deals together on the mainland. They had sold a small development of villas together as co-brokers. As she talked, she reached into her leather tote bag and pulled out a presentation folder, embossed with her name.

"Apologies, team, but I did not prepare one for each of you. However, I noted a few things I thought would facilitate our discussion today. Page 1 includes all our past transactions, organized by property address, where Carl and I worked together. The following page has a list of properties we were considering as potential flips—some here and some on the mainland. Of course, we couldn't do them all at once. We had to prioritize. Do you see the ones in the bold font? Those were our top contenders, the ones we were seriously considering purchasing with the intent of fixing up and reselling quickly. There are two here on the island."

At Julie's direction, Cole drove us to the first property, which was at the opposite end of the island, about a ten-minute drive. Unprompted, Theresa described the dinner she shared with Carl where they each realized there was more going on between them than their work. As she told the story, they simply evolved into a romantic couple.

"It was natural," she said. "Little by little, we spent more time together and we saw things the same way. We both liked watching college football, we liked thriller movies, and we always had something to talk about. So, we spent more and more time together. It was easy to be with Carl and, surprisingly, he found it easy to be with me. People don't always say that about me, for some reason." She sat a little straighter as she finished speaking, like admitting this unburdened her from something she usually hides.

We pulled into a dirt driveway. In front of us was a small cottage that clearly needed substantial renovations, set far back from the road.

"You're right," I said. "This is a hidden treasure."

"Carl was very good at finding these gems. He knew the owner and had been talking to him, working with him for at least six months. Most likely, we would have to completely gut the interior, but we thought we could get it for the right price to make the numbers work."

"I can see what you saw in this place," I said, looking around the property.

"We wanted this one because of its location. It's pretty secluded back here, so a new buyer wouldn't have to deal with all the tourists and their nonsense. The county dock is right down the road, which is perfect for people who want to get in and out of here without riding with a hundred or so people crammed onto a ferry. Since it is on the opposite side of the island, far away from the other dock, it definitely feels more remote, right?"

These did not seem to be the words of someone emotionally tied to this island, someone who put up with inconveniences because the payoff of living here, of being here, was worth it. This sounded like she had already done a cost-benefit analysis and fortunately, this property ended up on the right side of her balance sheet.

Deputy Julie and Lieutenant Cole had their own questions and their own rhythm of asking them. Theresa wove her story about the weeks leading up to last Saturday like someone working on a needlepoint. Her thread was going in and out of this fabric, creating this design as she spoke. There were colors of different events and conversations creating an image.

But was it real? The parts and pieces of this story sounded very much like she and Carl were a couple, who shared many interests, including this island and selling real estate on it. The more she talked, though, the main difference between them also became clear. Carl wanted to sell property here because he loved Mongin Island. It made him happy when other people chose to spend a part of their lives here.

He believed in all of it: the beautiful beachfront properties and the tiny cottages, the dirt roads and fishing from the dock, the history, the idea of being part of the community. With half our tour over, the only thing Theresa had convinced me of was that she believed in the lucrative deals she and Carl were able to broker.

"Honestly, that is amazing, Theresa. In a way, I'm finding one detail actually very hard to believe," Julie said. "Real estate sales are so emotional. Large purchases and lots of change are definitely a recipe for short fuses. And you're saying Carl never had this experience? Every client was just as happy as a June bug?" Julie turned from the front passenger seat to look at Theresa directly and pulled her long hair behind her right shoulder so she could get a better look at her. Their eyes locked. I was caught off guard that Julie suddenly changed the meeting's energy with just a few words.

"Well, yes, you don't have to believe me, I guess. Call his clients, everything is in his database. He has every client and all his transactions, and he kept a log of all his showings, open houses, everything. You don't need me to tell you this, you can find it yourself." She took Julie's challenge.

"My team is doing exactly that, as we speak," Julie said.

"If Carl had clients who were upset with him, I don't know who they are," Theresa said. "I never met one, never heard him talk about a bad client situation. Of course, there were sticking points in some deals, but no show-stoppers, no deals that fell through. Carl got his deals done and got paid." She answered without breaking eye contact, not backing down from the implications Julie was making.

I was so engrossed in this exchange that the road to the next destination passed without me noticing. In no time, we arrived at a modest house very close to the island church, right in the middle of the island. We climbed out and walked to the front of the car. Deputy Julie leaned against the bumper, her left elbow rested on the hood. Her posture was relaxed but her eyes were alert, focused on all that was going on around us.

From the outside, the house looked in decent shape. With a fresh coat of paint and some yard work, this house would definitely have curb appeal. Theresa was explaining the owner had moved to an assisted living community on the mainland but his children wanted to sell. Disagreements between the family kept them from moving forward.

"It's a classic example of why families should not leave properties vacant," Theresa explained. "They're driving their own price down by not maintaining the property. Carl had just about convinced them to agree on our price and to sell. We told them we would make them an all-cash offer."

Our conversation was interrupted by the rattle of a golf cart hitting the bumps in the uneven dirt road. Over Deputy Julie's shoulder, I watched Missy approach, not sure what to do or say.

"What did you do to him, what did you do?" Missy shouted at Theresa as she climbed out of the cart. In just a couple of strides, she had elbowed her way into our circle. Theresa recoiled as she shook her head from side to side.

"Everything was fine until you came along! What did you do!?" Missy continued to scream. Julie stepped forward, positioning herself at Missy's side.

"Missy, I am going to have to ask you to take a few steps back, now," Julie commanded, but instead, Theresa complied. Cole had already moved to stand on Missy's other side. Both officers were ready if this escalated.

"I'm sorry, but I don't—" Theresa began.

"Sorry? You're sorry? Carl is dead because of you! You couldn't leave him alone. You had to ruin everything!" Missy looked at Theresa with white-hot hatred.

"I didn't do anything," Theresa said. "Look, I don't know what you think I did, but I can assure you, I didn't do it!" Theresa had backed up until she was close to me.

"Missy, please," I said, as I raised my hands in the air. "This is not helping Carl. We are trying to figure out what happened to him, you know that. Theresa is telling us about some of the work they were doing."

"So, you're just going to stand there, you're just going to allow her to stand there and you're not doing anything to her? She gets away with this?" Missy shifted her anger to Julie and then Cole, daring them to punish Theresa. Had Missy actually seen more than she shared with me?

My thoughts were trying to catch up to Missy, but she refocused on Theresa and with new energy, she demanded, "Why couldn't you just have left him alone? It was all your stupid idea to find a buyer for Governor's Point. You greedy, wicked woman!" Missy looked at each one of us, her eyes wide and the vein on her temple bulging.

"I don't know who you are or what you want, but whatever it is, you definitely have the wrong person. Still, I hope you find your answer," Theresa said, I think trying to sound more confident than she felt. She smoothed her hair and straightened her top while looking at Missy.

"What the—now you're just going to pretend? You fake, miserable, terrible woman. You are a horrible excuse for a girlfriend. He actually felt something for you? You fake, awful—" Missy was hurling insults like a pitching machine on the fritz. The show was over though, according to Deputy Julie, who firmly took her by the arm and pushed her toward her cart.

"Enough now, Missy. Let's go," Julie commanded.

"Missy, go along now and cool off, you settle yourself down before something else goes wrong." Deputy Julie directed Missy to her cart, where fortunately Missy climbed in without resisting. "You head along now, and we will say this little show of yours never happened. You may be upset now, but you are dangerously close to interfering with police business," Julie said sharply, "I don't need you tracking us down and inserting yourself."

"Tracking you down? Please," she scoffed, "you're out here for all the world to see. The whole island is talking about you dragging her here, and how she is your prime suspect," Missy snapped.

Lieutenant Cole appeared around the passenger side of Missy's cart. "Go ahead Missy, we can take it from here. Do yourself and us a favor and let us get back to it," he said.

After one last piercing leer at Theresa, Missy shot me a look that, if I read it correctly, conveyed a betrayal. She put her cart into reverse and without looking, backed up, turned quickly onto School Road and headed toward the church. We all stood silently for a moment, absorbing the chaos, the absurdity of what we witnessed, what was said, and what was left unsaid.

Theresa's stunned expression revealed that Missy's outburst had penetrated her cool, collected demeanor. She was rattled. "Who was that?" she whispered, wiping the sweat from her upper lip with her left hand.

"What do you mean?" I asked as Julie and Cole rejoined us.

"Theresa, are you alright?" Julie asked. "Do you need a few minutes before we continue?"

"I can continue, yes, but who was that woman?" Theresa asked again.

"You really don't know who that was?" Julie asked.

"No clue. What was her name? Missy? I couldn't even understand what was being said, it all happened so fast. How does she know me?" Theresa's eyes searched our faces as if asking us to pick her side. But her side of what, exactly?

"Yes, that was Missy," Julie said, then waited for a response.

"Missy who?" Theresa demanded.

"Missy was previously in a relationship with Carl. Carr, can you fill Theresa in?" Julie said.

"From what I gather, Missy and Carl were casually dating until very recently, when Carl apparently ended it with Missy. She had told him that she was allergic to his dog Buddy—and shortly after that Carl stopped speaking to Missy. Next thing we know, you and Carl are seen out and about together."

"How recently?" Theresa asked.

"Missy said their relationship ended a few weeks ago."

"So essentially, what you're saying is, there was a time when he was involved with both of us. Missy knew about me, but Carl never mentioned her, I had no idea. What a fool I was." Theresa said sadly, unaware of the irony that Missy shared her same words and feelings.

"Missy thinks I had something to do with Carl's death because I appeared in Carl's life at the same time as interest in Governor's Point heated up? Well, I didn't. I can tell you that. I may not have known about her but I absolutely had nothing to do with Governor's Point. That deal was all Carl. After all this time, he had not one, but two people showing interest in the property."

"Two parties interested in Governor's Point?" Julie asked.

Cole was writing in the small notebook he carried.

"Yes, there was one group, some foreign investor who Carl, I think, connected to the developer. I know Carl had been spending a lot of time with this guy recently and they were all supposed to meet to walk the property. Carl said this guy was interested in building sustainably. I guess he wanted to talk to the developer to see if they could minimize the construction's environmental impact. He wanted to consider doing some off-site construction and framing that would be transported by boat to the site. It would be expensive, but this investor wanted property owners who would buy into this. Carl wondered how the few landowners already here would feel about this idea."

Theresa was regaining her composure. Talking about business centered her.

"So, he did tell you some things," Julie said.

"Just that vague outline," Theresa said.

"How about names?" Julie asked. "We're working through Carl's files, but we're still looking for names on this deal."

Theresa shook her head. "No, Carl did not share that with me, because it wasn't my deal. I didn't ask. He did tell me that he was under a nondisclosure agreement."

"So, what about this other interested party?" Julie prompted.

"Carl only told me this guy was foreign and a bit of a hothead. He presented an interesting proposal, a property trade. Realtors were doing some of those deals here about ten years ago. There are some houses here that were swapped for better pieces of land back then, but I haven't seen that since the market cooled off. Brokers used to like trading because it was fast, easy, and deals closed quickly."

Now, I was even more curious. I asked, "Are you saying this other interested party had property on the island that he wanted to trade for Governor's Point? Did Scott Campino know about this?"

"I don't know for sure, but I don't think so," Theresa said. "I think Carl was still vetting it. I recall he said the other property was beachfront, too. From the little I know, though, Scott would be wise to make the deal if we can still make it happen."

Theresa was showing signs of fatigue. She looked at her watch. "Will I still make the 5:00 boat? Should I push my reservation?"

"No, we can wrap up and get you on that boat, but we have a little more time before we need to head back to the dock," Julie said. "If we drove down Beach Road, would you be able to point out what land was part of this potential trade?"

"Highly unlikely," Theresa said. "He mentioned it once as we were driving, and I recall it being on the right side of the road, but I was not really paying close attention."

As Lieutenant Cole drove back to the ferry landing, Julie and Theresa made plans for a follow-up discussion. Theresa sprang out of the car almost as soon as it came to a stop back at the gangway. "I hope today was helpful for you," Theresa called out loudly, as if her energy had been magically restored and she wanted everyone in earshot to hear.

Julie did not answer her, which I noticed was a pattern of hers. She simply shook Theresa's hand and thanked her for her time. Theresa smiled and turned to join the line forming on the dock. She popped a pair of earphones in and was absorbed into the crowd. As far as she was concerned, the visit was officially over.

As we stood watching her board, I said, "Wow, Julie! I feel like we learned a lot today, but I've still got more questions than answers."

"What's bothering you most? If you had to pick one thing, what would it be?" Julie asked as I got behind the wheel of my cart.

"Definitely Missy," I said. "She surprised me, to say the least. All that drama seemed way over the top for someone who was casually dating Carl. I get that Missy is angry about the other woman, but for Pete's sake, Carl and Missy had just started dating. They weren't married for years and years. Just two days ago, we sat together and she told me she did not expect a serious relationship with Carl. Fast forward to today: Where did all that emotion come from? It was like a completely different Missy showed up. In the time I spent with her alone, Missy blamed Theresa for breaking them up—but not for hurting Carl. And here we are, today, and she is implying Theresa may have killed him. I can't help but think she saw more than she is letting on. I was just so surprised today. I saw flashes of her temper with me, which I understood. But today was next level."

"To be honest, Carr, I thought we were going to end up detaining her. She was a minute or two away from me putting some cuffs on her. I wanted her to make the decision to back down herself, but I was prepared to remove her, if we had to. And, I agree with you, something doesn't add up here."

"I wish we knew exactly where she was on the island on Thursday," I said.

"You're right, we have no footage of Missy anywhere last Thursday that would lead to Governor's Point. The island doesn't have that many cameras. Just the landing, the fire station, the church, the Inn, and the coffee shop. So, as far as we know, she was at home all day, like she said. We will spend some time to find out about Missy's history. No one here seems to know her well, so I wonder if the behavior we just witnessed is part of a pattern of instability. I agree, today felt like a performance of some kind, to me anyway."

Theresa's visit was supposed to provide a direction forward but instead, we were left with a haze over the facts of the case that previously seemed clear.

"I also have more questions about Theresa," I said. "She seems to have had so much in common with Carl, but is that true? Seems like they shared some interests, I guess, but their perspective on Mongin Island and really, on selling properties here, seems as far apart as you could get. The community on Mongin Island was important to Carl. He was a fixture here and a part of a lot of lives. It seems odd that he would be attracted to someone who viewed our island just as a revenue stream."

"That's fair," Julie agreed. "I noticed the same thing. Carl was successful on this island because he sold the experience, he sold the idea of living here, and people connected with that. Everyone we've talked to so far said this about him. But when you put it all together, I don't think that is a reason to doubt Theresa. So far, everything she said is accurate and can be verified. And she has an alibi for Thursday. If I've learned one thing in this job, it's that things sometimes are not as complicated as we try to make them. So far, I can't see Theresa as a murderer."

"Right. She wasn't even here on Thursday," I said. "But we still don't know the exact time of death, do we?"

"No, the body having been immersed in all those chemicals and who knows what in that pool water makes a time-of-death trickier to determine, but we should have that report soon," Julie said.

After making plans to talk again tomorrow, we parted ways.

I was driving back to Books & Brew as the events of the day registered all at once. I realized I was physically and mentally drained. In one morning, relationships were strengthened and they were tested, facts were confirmed and they were questioned. Today was just one day, and it was one hundred days. We had made progress today. Tomorrow we would begin putting these pieces together.

Chapter 18

That night, the rest I sought, that I needed, eluded me. All the usual tricks I use to invite sleep failed me. Dinner, a brisk walk on the beach, a warm bath, and a cup of steaming chamomile tea tricked me into falling asleep quickly at first—but all too soon I was wide awake, sitting at my kitchen table three hours before my alarm was set to ring. All that was said yesterday and more that went unspoken replayed in my head. I felt as though I was looking for something that was already known to me. Governor's Point, previously abandoned and forgotten, was the star of our island show now.

Buddy faithfully settled under my chair with his eyes sealed shut, his head rested on his two crossed paws.

"Come on sweetheart, if you have to be out of bed, you should at least be comfortable." We moved together to the sofa. Buddy curled into his usual donut. I wrapped him in the cozy, chenille throw that rested on the back of the sofa and opened my laptop. "Buddy my boy, we are going to find out what large parcels line Beach Road and then we are going to find out who owns them." At the sound of his name, Buddy gave a soft, encouraging thump of his tail while I opened the county's property database.

As night faded, my vision for the day became brighter, almost as if the rising sun burned away the chaos and confusion of the past few days. With the sky painted in shades of blue and pink, today held promise. My notebook was filled with today's agenda items and although it was early, I decided to get a start on the day.

After a quick stop at the General Store for a couple of carrot and raisin muffins, I arrived at Books & Brew. The store was also ready for a full day, thanks to Tripp's hard work yesterday. Brewing a fresh carafe of English breakfast tea, I placed our baked goods on the back counter and waited for him to arrive. The quiet was interrupted by my cell phone chiming from the bottom of my tote bag.

"I bet you that's Tripp, telling us he is on his way," I told Buddy. Digging my phone out, I instead found Missy's text waiting for me.

The lone word on the screen was: "Sorry."

It took me a minute to decide how to answer her. The apology was appreciated, sure, but what was she sorry for: the way she acted, the things she said, all of it? Did I want to have this conversation by text? Would she be willing to put her thoughts in writing?

I'm not ready to do this with her, I thought. So, I responded simply, honestly: "I hope you feel better today."

Missy did not answer, leaving me with my unanswered questions.

The day's first agenda item was reaching Bob and Monica. Time to eat some pie that was never going to be on Miss Lucy's menu: humble pie. Maybe my anxiety about what I had not told Bob and Monica was one thing that kept me up last night. I drafted this email in my head dozens of times. Now it was time to just write and send.

My phone rang shortly after hitting send and I felt a rush of anxiety seeing the name on the screen's display.

"Good morning, Bob."

"Is it?"

I cringed.

"Got your email, just now, and well, Carr, this is a small world and stories and requests travel fast. We are a strong network. Of course I know Monica, and it didn't take too long for us to see that we were tripping over each other—that we shared a contact."

"Bob, I don't know what to say. Are you very upset? I can't tell."

"I was annoyed, yes, and so was Monica. More than that, I guess, we were not happy to be treated unprofessionally. We both responded to you, to try to offer our services and broker this deal for you. But not to worry, Carr. We have moved on from being annoyed with you to being disappointed that this was all a big waste of time. We get that you are new to this, so rather than ruin what can be a very long, strong relationship, we were going to talk to you. You beat us to it, Carr. In this business, everyone knows everyone. You would be much better served by being direct with us."

He paused and it took me a moment to respond. "Bob, I am disappointed in myself, honestly. It didn't feel right to keep this information from you both. Ultimately, I am a beginner, but I knew better and I apologize. This isn't the first time this week I got off track. I didn't mean to pit you both against each other, but I see now that I did and that's wrong. I hope you and Monica can forgive me."

"Already done, for me, anyway, and actually Monica is a lot nicer than me." He laughed gently. "Give her a call, smooth it over, and we will call it a beginner's mistake. Thank you for your note, I know you feel badly and I appreciate you coming clean, owning it. Let's put it behind us."

"You're right, I'm just finding my way in this business. I thought that I was just putting out some regular inquiries about some rare books but—as we now know—I had no idea how rare that one book was."

"This business really is a community of friends. We see each other at conferences. We compare notes. We chat. I won't lie to you, sometimes we do compete for business, but mostly we all want to see each other succeed. We want people to keep reading and buying books."

"I get it, Bob. Please let me treat you and Monica to dinner at the Inn when you're in the area again. It is the very least I can do."

"Now that's an offer I know we won't refuse. Thank you," he said. "Not only did Monica and I burn up hours on this—but it turned out to be a dead end!"

"Tell me about that," I said. "This mystery man didn't have the book anymore?"

"No, now he is saying he has agreed to make a substantial donation of rare books, including that particular series, to the Library of Congress, but he didn't share any other details. It's like the book has just gone—poof. Gone just like that." I heard him snap his fingers.

"What a roller coaster ride. This donation just happened?"

"Yeah. Recently—I think. I'm not exactly sure of the dates. I guess the good news is that your customer eventually will get what he wants, which is access."

"But how long does that whole process take?"

"I wouldn't imagine any time soon, that's for sure, but who can tell? Maybe by next year they'll be accessible."

I was jotting notes to share with Paul.

Bob kept going. "But maybe all is not lost. I did find one other book on your customer's list, one that was easy to find—and I put that in the mail to you. You'll at least have something for your customer and hopefully it serves him well."

"Thank you, Bob, that was very kind of you to do that for me. Let me know how much I owe you for that."

Bob asked me about my family and remembered to ask about Tripp before we hung up. But the directness of his call left me grappling with my imposter syndrome once again. What was I doing, trying to help track down a killer, when my own business skills weren't even up to the basics? That hit hard. I had slipped up, big time. This was definitely a low point. I thought back over that day I called Monica and Bob and realized that I should have told them more. I called Monica immediately and left her an apology on her voicemail.

Once Tripp arrived and we ate breakfast, our day was planned in no time. He agreed to watch the store while he worked on the website, and I was going to explore the parcels on Beach Road.

"I wonder if Barb has some time to spend cruising around with me," I said as Tripp cleared up our breakfast plates and cups.

"I guess you can ask her yourself, she is knocking on the front door!" Tripp said.

"Hey, y'all!" Barb greeted us with a big smile and a few papers in her right hand. "I have here today's blog post by Darcy Meadows from *The Island Insider*. Guess who is your newest fan?"

"Darcy, from the tourism group? Wow," I said, opening one of her papers.

"Carr, she has a huge following," Tripp said. "She posts a few times a week and she has put quite a few local places on the map, particularly over on the mainland. This could be really big for us—I mean, you. This could be really big for you."

"Definitely could be big for us, Tripp—for all of us. This would not be happening without you both." I read quickly. "This post is great. I mean, she understood what we are doing here, Tripp. People can see it and feel it!"

We took a few more minutes to digest this unexpected good news.

"Barb, you caught me right before I texted you," I said. "Do you feel like doing a little exploring with me today? So much has happened since I last saw you. I have to bring you up to speed and I don't even know where to begin, really." We said goodbye to Tripp and Buddy and were soon on our way to Beach Road. Barb listened quietly as I relayed yesterday's events.

I was nowhere near done recounting all of it when we arrived at the intersection of School Road and Beach Road.

Barb set our course, "Let's go down to the beach and then work our way back up the road, looking at the parcels on the right side."

I agreed. "Good idea. There are three lots I want to explore and I also found one on the left side of the road we probably should look at, just in case Theresa got mixed up. All four of these lots have different owners listed on the deeds. I would like to get a better sense of what a potential buyer saw. I want to see which ones might match Governor's Point and be considered for a swap. Theresa said Scott would be a fool not to make the swap—so the property here would have to be at least as marketable or probably, better than Governor's Point, right?"

"That makes sense," Barb said, "but after seeing Governor's Point—how are any of these lots as good or better than that?" Barb looked carefully at the land on both sides of this dirt road. "I am not seeing it!" She folded her arms across her chest.

"Well, here we go!" I said as I made a U-turn in the parking lot at the beach. It became clear, relatively quickly, that this task was going to be more challenging in person than on paper. I had the site comparisons jotted down, but as we drove up to the first selection, it was anyone's best guess where the property lines were. Without that, it was hard to make a comparison to Governor's Point.

"So, this might be a waste of time, or worse—one of my dumber ideas," I said sadly. "Seems I might be striking out everywhere today."

"Nonsense, come on, pull over here," Barb said, pointing to a flat area next to Beach Road. On some other roadway, it might have served as a breakdown lane. Here, it was a sparsely grassy patch where you could see sand peeking through. "Time to get some steps in!" Barb said as she hopped out of the cart and climbed the small embankment that lined the lot.

There was no clearing, no already-made path. This did not stop Barb. She forged forward, gently patting the tree trunks she passed. I followed dutifully, looking for something that would stand out, something that would convince Scott to trade the land in which he had already invested. We reached a clearing shaded by tall pine trees. Their fallen needles created a brown carpet that covered our shoes.

"Well, it looks like the county GIS maps were right," Barb said. "There is no water here, no pond, no lake. It's relatively flat, to the point that not much grading would be needed. I know I'm not the best judge because I'm biased, but this is no Governor's Point."

I had to agree. It was a nice piece of land, and although we certainly hadn't seen it all, it was no Governor's Point. There was no magic, no mystery, no seclusion. Once houses were built here, it would be just another neighborhood. You certainly would not drive down a bumpy road in the middle of the woods to happen upon this parcel. Are any of these lots on Beach Road going to be a Governor's Point?

"How could Theresa think this potential trade was a smart deal?" I asked.

"Maybe it's because she doesn't care about all those things that make Governor's Point special," Barb said. "It's possible she saw property near the beach and, in her mind, that equals a good deal to her. She probably thought they could spin this as 'almost beachfront' or some other marketing mumbo-jumbo and that would justify high-priced sales."

Barb continued. "This doesn't feel like it, though. This doesn't feel like a good trade for Governor's Point." In agreement, we followed the same self-made path back to the cart.

"Onward!" Barb declared before I could talk her out of continuing. I smiled. She knew me well. Everyone should have a Barb in their life. She knew my confidence was low and that I was still reeling from my own disappointment in myself.

I complied and drove a few hundred feet down the road.

"I think this is it, or close to it," I said as we came to a stop. From the road, this parcel appeared flatter. "It looks like this area over there could be a cut-through to whatever is behind this, you know, like what people did on the side of our lot. People used that strip of land between our lot and our neighbors, rather than just drive all around the resort to get to the Inn. Looks like the same thing is going on there."

"Want to drive up there or just walk?" Barb asked. We agreed to walk and followed this small path directly into a clearing you couldn't see from the road. This area, hidden by the trees and brush, was flat and gave us a complete 360-degree view.

"Of course, it would depend on the soil composition around here, but this looks like a great place to build," Barb said softly. As island residents, we were both aware of the dreaded, nerve-wracking soil test mandated in this area, the results of which determined the required height of the pylons on which your house sat. The sandier the soil, the more reinforcements you needed, which meant higher building expenses.

We were standing next to each other, so our eyes came to rest on the same thing at the same time, off to the right of this clearing. We turned to each other.

"That looks out of place, here, right?" Barb asked me. She was pointing to the flattened pampas grasses, trampled brush, and broken branches. It was an area about fifteen feet wide and definitely had been disturbed recently. The hairs on my arms were standing up.

Barb pointed to a large brown circle on the ground next to the flattest patch. "Oh Carr, do you think this is blood?"

I was stunned. "It certainly looks like it, but maybe it's from an animal."

As we got closer, we instinctively kept our hands at our sides, trying not to disturb anything.

"Barb, I don't think it belongs to an animal. Look over there, over where the land dips down. What's that white thing, right there?"

I ran forward and she followed. We dug the tips of our feet into the ground at the edge of the clearing as it abruptly sloped down. Our eyes found an off-white, standard golf cart resting on its passenger side. The very tip of its roof reached above the top of the clearing.

"Oh my God," I said.

And Barb said simply, "Carl."

Chapter 19

Neither of us had cell phone reception this far into the woods, so we ran quickly back to my cart, still parked on Beach Road. Julie answered on the first ring and said she and her team would meet us at the site in under forty minutes. She didn't ask a lot of questions after she heard the two key pieces of information: a found cart and a possible bloodstain.

I sat behind the steering wheel, with my legs dangling over the cart's side.

Barb paced along the side of the road, debating aloud. "You know, it might not be Carl's. A lot of carts disappear, especially the rental ones. You said it yourself, a lot of carts look identical to each other."

A moment later, she said, "Also, who knows how long it has been there? It could have been there for days, weeks, we don't know."

I let her talk and pace. Finally, she leaned against the metal frame herself and I said, "Barb, I think we have to accept the fact that this could be Carl's cart and we might be one step closer to the truth. This is what we want, right? We want to find out the truth. We want this behind us, right?"

"You're right, I know. Regardless of whether this is Carl's cart or not, he is still dead and someone needs to be held accountable. I know that sounds awful, but it is true. We want that person off this island if he or she is still here. You're right," Barb responded, took several deeper breaths, and closed her eyes.

We remained just like that, in the silence of true friends. No more words were necessary or spoken.

True to her promise, Julie and a whole calvary of experts arrived. The familiar black Tahoe kicked up dust as it drove toward us. We did not see the smaller white Chevy Blazer following in its path until it pulled up in front of us. Doors opened, people piled out, and the lift-gate doors were raised. In a matter of minutes, supplies were grabbed, teams were suited up, and the professionals got to work. Barb and I quickly led them to the area and then stepped back to let them gather evidence.

Barb and I were walking back to my cart when I heard Julie's voice calling my name: "Carr, hold up!" She jogged over to us. "We will be here for hours, and we are a long way from knowing anything defin-itive, but we found a windbreaker underneath the cart. Chances are it was on the front seat when the cart tipped over. It's navy blue and has the Mongin Island lighthouse logo on the front, right side. Could belong to anyone—maybe someone bought it in the gift shop, I know. But I wanted you to have that piece of information."

Julie looked solemnly at us. Barb and I both understood what she was telling us, and Julie gave us a minute to absorb it. This was very likely where Carl was either seriously injured or where he was killed. I appreciated her breaking this news to us gently.

I decided to share some of what I had found. "Julie, according to the county records, this land is owned by a limited liability corporation called Mongin Properties 17 LLC. It was incorporated in Delaware but is registered here, in South Carolina. The agent of record is an attorney in Charleston. When I was researching this morning, that's as far as I could get. I could call this attorney. I am not sure if he will speak to me, but I can do that if you want."

"Yes, if you will take the first pass, that would be great. When we finish here, I will give you a call and we can see where we both end up. Thank you both for your help today and please, keep this as quiet as possible. I will be moving our vehicles up to the first clearing. Don't want or need a crowd traipsing around on any potential evidence."

She jogged down to the Blazer, climbed in, and started it. We returned to my cart and sat quietly for a few minutes as Julie repositioned her vehicles.

Barb spoke first. "I have to say, I guess, I didn't really think it was a possibility. I just never expected to be at the exact spot where some-one—a person—I mean, Carl, died. I just never thought about it."

"That makes two of us," I said. "I thought we were going to walk around these parcels and get some kind of a feeling, telling us which was the best match. I thought we would be out here for thirty minutes, maybe an hour at most, and then we would be on our way, armed with knowing what Carl saw in a potential trade. Poor Carl, seeing the blood and the branches, the grass, the land all disturbed—his last minutes must have been terrifying and painful."

"But *how* did Carl's body end up at Governor's Point?" Barb asked.

"And *why* did he end up at Governor's Point? What is the connection?" I mused.

"Let's swing by my house, I can call the attorney from there and we can regroup," I said. Barb nodded.

A few minutes later we were in my kitchen. I poured us each a tall glass of sweet tea while Barb went to splash cool water on her face. I grabbed my notebook and we sat at my kitchen table to dial the contact number listed online for the LLC.

"Here goes nothing and everything," I said to Barb as the phone rang.

My call was answered by a friendly, female voice who told me Mr. Parker Taylor was currently unavailable. Fortunately, Mr. Taylor had a brief window for returning calls in approximately thirty minutes. Would that work for my schedule? I politely agreed. Barb and I waited at the table as the minutes passed by, marked by the steady ticking of my pendulum wall clock. Its rhythm filled our silence and competed with the noise of the thoughts in our heads.

We tossed around a few strategies for my approach to Taylor. Should I be cagey with the reason for my call and only provide the most basic information? Should I tell him everything going on here on the island and break the news that those involved with his LLC will be answering questions about a newly discovered crime scene? Our third option was to invent some fictitious ruse, like potentially being interested in purchasing a nearby parcel and wanting to know more about the neighbors. There was no clear winner. We quickly agreed Mr. Taylor, as an attorney, was likely very skilled in gathering information without providing any to us. We decided we would share enough of what was happening here in the hope he would be curious for more details. Then I would ask about the parties who set up the limited liability corporation and hopefully he would answer because he would want the rest of our story. We would offer a verbal quid pro quo, so to speak.

And, of course, we kept returning to the scene of the crime. At one point, Barb asked, "How did you even see those couple of inches of white sticking over the ledge?"

"It was just something in the corner of my eye. Maybe I was just meant to see it."

"And now—" Barb said, "Now we have to figure out how Carl got from Beach Road to Governor's Point and also, how did this happen without anyone else seeing it?"

"Well, I think we can rule out Carl being transported in a truck or car because I didn't see any tire tracks. We would have seen those as we climbed into the clearing today. I didn't see any—unless I missed them. I think we should go back and look more closely at Governor's Point, see if we can find tracks and maybe footprints. I know Julie's team took tire casts and pictures. But I think we should see it again, with fresh eyes. Maybe that will help us figure out how Carl got there and what the connection is."

I hadn't realized I felt so strongly about it until I made this declaration. "I think we should go today," I said.

Before Barb could answer, my cell phone rang. I answered on the second ring. "Hello, Mr. Taylor?"

"Yes, hello, apologies for the delay in getting to you. How can I help you? The note I have indicates an interest in a limited liability corporation. Tell me about your business and how I can help."

Our carefully laid plan went along well until the point when I asked for his client's name.

"Am I to understand there has potentially been a crime committed on the property in question? And to be clear, we are speaking about the approximately twenty acres located on Beach Road? Let me get the property ID number here from the deed, hold on please."

After listening to his keyboard clicking, he read the same long number I pulled from the county website. I confirmed the number. He said nothing. I held my breath and waited for him.

The silence was broken, "So essentially, you want to find out who is behind this LLC? Unfortunately, you will have to register with the South Carolina Secretary of State and request the registration documents directly from them. Those documents will include the articles of incorporation. You can also try the Delaware Secretary of State as you likely know that is where this particular entity was formed. Same deal there. There is a small fee for the documents, wherever you request them, but nothing onerous. In the meantime, I will advise my client to answer questions asked in an official capacity by law enforcement."

Clearly, by that, he meant: Not us.

"I understand," I said, "but this request is obviously time sensitive and frankly, a matter of public safety."

"Bring me a court order and I will happily comply," he said. There was a smugness in his tone. Ever so slightly, I heard the tone of a small victory. "Until then, I assume, this conversation has concluded, unless, of course, there is another matter on which I can be of assistance."

Another matter? I almost snapped: How about *this* matter? Instead, I thanked him for doing basically nothing, and our call ended.

"Well, that was equal parts a waste of time and infuriating," I said to Barb, as I placed the phone on the table. "But I have an idea—let's see if I am right." I turned to my laptop and logged into the data vault containing Carl's files.

"We probably should have gone with the fake neighbor story." Barb half smiled. As I tapped on my laptop, she asked, "Are you thinking that Carl already has a history with this property? Before he was approached about the potential swap?" She scooted her chair closer to mine so she could see my screen.

"That's exactly what I'm thinking. Everyone has said Carl was often on both sides of a sale and that he sold some properties multiple times. Maybe this is also one of those deals, right? I don't know why I didn't dig into these files first."

It took only a few minutes to navigate to Carl's historical records. "Bless his heart, he was organized!" With a couple of taps, I found the correct transaction year and searched the spreadsheet for the property ID. "Well, Mr. Parker Taylor, it turns out we don't need you after all."

With wide eyes, I looked at Barb and asked hopefully, "Do you happen to know an Amelia Burke?"

Chapter 20

Barb turned to look out my kitchen window as she searched her memory bank. "The name is familiar to me, but I can't place it," she finally said. "I'm actually thinking that's the name of an old friend from college or maybe an author I've read. I've got nothing, really."

I nodded as I continued searching Carl's files for any other Amelia Burke reference. I agreed it seemed like a name I had heard before.

"Carr, if you want to go to Governor's Point, I think we should go soon. I have guests arriving later today on the 4:00 boat. I need to be available for them. And don't even think about going out there by yourself."

I looked up to find her looking at me sternly, her eyebrows knitted together.

I reassured her, "Even if I wanted to, I doubt I would ever find my way down those twists and turns by myself!"

"That may be the only thing that saves us from you heading off by yourself at all hours."

We hit the road with a packed lunch, my camera, and a few supplies stuffed into my big canvas tote bag. "I feel like a real-life detective!" Barb laughed as we climbed into my cart.

We rode in silence, each lost in our thoughts. We turned off Old Port Passage Way to start down the dirt road into the woods.

"What happened to our sunny day?" I wondered aloud, "Is it supposed to rain?"

"This morning's weather report said clouds would roll in, but I thought it was supposed to be later. Gray skies do add a certain level of—I don't know, should we call it atmosphere?"

"I think we could both do without any more atmosphere, right?"

As the air filled with humidity, we could feel rain coming. We were back at the scene for the first time since Saturday, and all of our senses were on edge. Our surroundings seemed heavy with loss, fear, anger, and mystery. Except for her directions, Barb said nothing else until we pulled into the parking space in front of the gate.

"On second thought, let's move this cart and park farther away, like over there," I said as I backed up and drove to a clearing. "I want to explore where the killer likely parked."

Barb's hands were firmly on her hips. "What are we looking for? How do you want to start?"

I responded slowly as I thought this through. "If we accept that Carl was likely killed or at least seriously hurt at the Beach Road property, then let's get into the mindset of someone who would have brought him here. So, where would you park if you had just killed someone?"

"Where would I park if I had just killed someone? Not here, that's for sure. I wouldn't want to be at Governor's Point. Remember, this is my special spot."

"Exactly, being here has to mean something," I agreed. "If someone brought Carl here, they would have parked as close as possible to the gate, right? As close as they could get to where they wanted to leave him. So the question is, why would someone move their victim here, to this place, where no one ever goes? Why not leave him where he was? It was secluded there, too. There has to be a connection. Governor's Point, specifically, is part of this."

I walked as I talked. "For now, my theory is that whoever left Carl here acted alone and needed a way to get out of these woods.

Walking is an option, but not an easy one. If that person drove Carl's cart here, how would they get back home? No, they had to use their own transportation."

I continued, "If we believe that Carl died mostly from the internal injuries and not the injury to his head, then he might not have died immediately. Let's say Carl could have been put into someone else's cart. I'm guessing someone brought him here for some significant reason. And then, watched him suffer and die. Poor Carl, it's all awful."

Our eyes looked over the property in front of us, noticing the remnants of the sheriff's department investigation. Police tape had marked a barrier around the pool deck, but some long strands had already fallen. This felt like it was our invitation.

"Julie's team has already been through this, Carr," Barb said, sounding skeptical. "Look at those piles of leaves they turned over—and paths they cleared off. I don't know what we are going to find that she has not already seen, documented, and probably discarded."

"You're probably right," I said. "It is just a hunch. There was so much going on Saturday, I'm not sure I saw everything clearly. Don't you think it is easier to *see* this place—the scene—without everyone running around here? So, let's start at the beginning, retracing what we think were the steps of whoever brought Carl here. I'm thinking it had to be one person, someone big who could lift Carl."

We started in the parking spaces closest to the gate. The overgrown grass and the untamed landscape presented their own challenges. It wasn't as easy as just looking carefully. We had to get down and focus. The few tools we brought with us were impractical. Everything was too unkept to use small hand rakes and trowels. We walked around, silent and hunched over, looking in the grass and weeds, moving things with our hands.

"What is this?" Barb said. She crouched down. Under some leaves was a tiny blue lighthouse charm. "Do you have those plastic sandwich bags in your tote? Can you get one?" she asked as she looked up at me.

Returning to her just a minute later, I said, "I have seen that before, but I can't remember where. Do you recognize it?"

"No, I don't think so. I mean, it is just an ordinary thing. There is nothing remarkable about it, right?" She used one bag as a glove while inserting the charm into another. She sealed it shut as she looked at me. "What are we doing? This seems like a bridge too far. We are crawling around, picking up random things, storing them in plastic bags? Who knows how long this charm has been here?"

"Stay with me Barb, please. We've come this far, please, just a little bit more. Don't you want to know for sure that no stone was left unturned?"

"Well, no," she said. "I don't think turning over stones and digging around in the weeds is what Julie had in mind when she asked us to help. I think the actual detectives did this already. Meanwhile, some crazy killer could be lurking around out in these woods and we are here alone."

I had not realized that Barb was scared. "Ohh, Barb," I said. "Do you really think someone has been hiding in the woods for the past five days waiting to kill us? I don't think this crime was random at all. I think someone wanted Carl dead and it has something to do with this property. Carl was the target. We aren't. We are going to figure it out—so, please stay with me, just a little longer."

I hoped Barb would understand that her presence gave me a strength I hadn't felt in a long time.

Barb sighed, loud enough for me to know she was losing patience with all of this. "When we are two old ladies, sitting in the rockers on your porch, we are going to remember this day, that's for sure. Carr, in all my years, I would have never guessed this is how I would spend my time on Mongin Island, crawling around Governor's Point."

She shook her head. "I guess I am not as much afraid as I am uneasy and maybe a little uncomfortable, emotionally and physically."

Chapter 21

Even though I wouldn't have admitted it or maybe because I didn't consciously feel it, I probably shared Barb's concerns on some level because I was flooded with relief when she said what she said. There was strength in numbers, and knowing someone felt the way you do. Also, having someone to bounce ideas off was enormously helpful.

We resumed our search. The area up to the gate and around the pool deck provided nothing significant. Admittedly, I was beginning to feel defeat creeping in. I thought seeing the property again, facing what had happened here would give us a chance to find something helpful.

After another thirty minutes and with the skies darkening overhead, I finally was willing to leave. "Turns out this was likely a fool's mission. Let's get out of here," I said to Barb as we straightened up and brushed the dirt from our shorts. I walked behind her as we left through the gate. Although I knew it would squeak, the creaking of those rusty hinges still made me jump. My nerves were on edge, too.

"Looks like you have some kind of a bug bite on your leg, Barb. It's pretty red. Does it hurt?"

She stopped and twisted her leg to get a better view, "This one? I didn't feel anything bite."

"Here, hold on, I will take a picture so you can see it better," I said as I got my phone out and crouched. "Wait, what's this?"

She was concerned, "Oh no! Do you think it's a tick bite?"

Barb's bug bite was momentarily forgotten as I pulled another plastic bag from my front pocket. To our left, about five feet from the gate was a small, silver oval, about the size of a quarter, etched with crossed golf clubs. On either side of the clubs were the initials G and C. As I placed this piece into one of the bags, I stood slowly to face Barb.

"This feels important," I said. "This does not look like it has been here long, do you agree?"

"One hundred percent, yes, but it could belong to anyone. Lots of people golf on the island—what if it fell off of someone's golf bag? What if someone was walking through here and …"

"Walking through a deserted neighborhood, miles away from a course, carrying their golf bag? Barb, come on." I shook my head. "This medallion is from a trophy or maybe someone's shoe, like a loafer or something."

"Well, okay, someone is walking through an abandoned neighborhood carrying their golf trophy?" Barb shot back.

"Touché, point taken. I don't know exactly what it is, but I think this is important. Makes me want to see what else is still here. We almost missed this. If I hadn't been crouching just now, I wouldn't have seen it. Guess we owe that blasted mosquito a bit of thanks."

We drove back to the store so Barb could pick up her cart. Our heads were spinning with all that happened since Barb first walked through the door that morning, announcing the store's appearance in the *Island Insider*. I knew Barb's guests were arriving soon.

"Hey, I will call you tomorrow morning and let you know what Julie has to say. Thanks for everything today, Barb," I said.

She climbed into her cart and looked over at me, "Sounds good. And—sorry, Carr, I know I could have been more supportive this afternoon. I'm not sure why, but this got to me today. Maybe it feels a little more real now that the pieces are slowly coming together. But I didn't mean to—well I shouldn't—take it out on you."

This woman could not be a better friend. "Barb, please, there's nothing to apologize for. I think we are both a little raw. It's not every day we uncover a crime scene. I think we are handling it all pretty well, all things considered! I wake up thinking about it, go to sleep thinking about it. I mean, I don't know what I would do if it wasn't for Tripp. I have hardly worked all week. He is carrying the lion's share of the work at the store. Now, be safe driving back and we'll catch up later!"

Her smile seemed forced, but she waved as she headed out of the lot.

As I walked into the store, it gave me comfort to see customers in all the different rooms, all the chairs filled. People were gathered around the Trading Floor's table and the scent of black tea, lemongrass, and honey filled the air. There was a positive energy that I welcomed, especially after all that happened today.

"Tripp, hi. How are things going?" I asked as I walked to the register. "The store looks amazing. You're doing such a great job. Thank you." My eyes found Buddy, who clearly had identified *his* chair. He was curled up into the same one as yesterday, and my thoughtful customers had not shooed him away. Both of his eyes were on me as I walked over to kiss the top of his head. His tail wagged like a magic wand, swirling away all the difficulties, the pain, and the confusion of the day.

"Hi, my sweet boy, have you behaved for Uncle Tripp?"

Tripp laughed. "Honestly, this dog could not be any better behaved. Except for a quick break outside and a couple of greetings to our regular customers, Buddy has been keeping that chair warm all day. A perfect gentleman, indeed. I think a few friends have slipped him some treats as well. I'm not sure about the rest of us, but it has been a great day for Buddy!"

"You need to head out and get some rest," I said. "You have been chained to this store all week. I appreciate all you have done. The store is clean and organized, everything looks great but you need to have some free time, too. And—I want to let you know that I think we are getting closer to figuring out what happened with Carl. I know you don't want the details, I just want you to know that we are making progress."

"I'm fine, Carr," he said. "And I don't mind finishing up here, really. You look like it has been quite a day! You look wiped out." He smiled as he said it, but I could see the concern in his face. "I'm happy to finish out the day. Thanks for the update on where things stand. It has only been a few days but man, I don't need to tell you how those few days feel."

"No, I insist you go," I said. "I don't want you to get sick of us!"

Tripp started collecting his phone, keys, and backpack. As he scratched Buddy's head, he said, "Okay, well before I go, you have a couple of messages on your desk. You should know, Paul Easton is looking for you. He stopped in twice today and called shortly after you left. Also, Julie called—said she couldn't get you on your cell."

I dug my phone out of the tote bag and, sure enough, now that I had better reception, there was the notification of Julie's call and a text from her that just said, "Please call."

"Want me to stay so you can return Julie's call?" Tripp asked.

I shook my head. "No, you get going, but thanks again for everything. We're all making real progress here."

Chapter 22

Julie answered on the first ring. "How did things go for you today, Carr?"

I told her there was quite a bit to cover, so we agreed to talk in person. "I still have customers and Tripp just left, but we can talk here if you want. I will just have to keep my eye out, in case someone needs me."

When Julie arrived about ten minutes later, there were still three customers in the store. We moved to the back office and Julie pulled a chair to my desk. With the weight of the day on both of us, the small space felt cramped. Julie's long legs were stretched out in front of her, crossed at the ankles, and she rubbed her face with her hands.

"Can I get you some tea or something? Something to perk us up?" I offered.

"Amazing! Yes, please," she said.

I returned a few minutes later with two of my blue and white speckled mugs filled with steaming black tea. I settled into my desk chair and said, "My preference would have been to have a nice oolong for this time of the day. But today, that isn't going to work. I don't know about you, but I need a jolt. My mind is racing, but my body is dragging. Usually, I worry caffeine in the afternoon will keep me up, but it feels like tonight is going to be a long night of research."

Over the rim of her mug, her eyes met mine. "Unfortunately, you're not in the company of a tea connoisseur here. I'm just happy to sit down and have something delicious. Thanks, Carr."

She sipped from her cup, then said, "Before you start recounting your day, there are few things you need to know. Let me see, here." She opened up a notebook filled with tiny neat block handwriting that looked almost like it had been typed. "First news is that the complete coroner's report came back. You know, we are pretty lucky, timing-wise. The county just opened these autopsy facilities at the start of this year. Before then, anything suspicious was sent to the medical university and it could take maybe eight days to get the report, if not longer. Now that we have this report, we can release the body to Carl's family, and they can make their arrangements. Although, by family, we are talking about a sister and a niece. From what we can tell, Carl hasn't seen or spoken to either of them in years, many years. They had almost no reaction to the news of his passing."

After she sipped her tea and turned to a new page, she went on, "The blood panels are clear of poisons and narcotics. The full toxicology report will be at least a week away, but I feel confident in this information." Julie looked up quickly and continued, "Time of death is not conclusive, but estimates are forty to fifty hours prior to removal from the water. Of course, this is based on Carl's liver temperature, the pool water temperature, and the atmospheric conditions. So, that puts his death somewhere early to mid-morning on Thursday, just as Missy suggested. The coroner confirmed that Carl died from the impact of blunt force trauma to the head, which caused his intracranial hemorrhaging. He has ruled this death a homicide.'" Julie sat back in her chair and finished. "Now, we know the time of death and the cause."

Carl's time and cause of death, spoken into existence here in my office, pulled it from the abstract to the profound. Until now, there was another possibility at every turn: Maybe it wasn't Carl, maybe it was accidental, maybe there was another, a better explanation than what all the signs were telling us. Now that the experts had weighed in, it was real in a way I had protected myself from fully accepting.

"It seems I am better at compartmentalizing than I thought," I said, breaking our silence. "My mind allowed me to hold on to other possibilities, explanations, I think. I don't know how you do this job, Julie, and face these things every single day."

"I don't want to say you get used to it, which sounds callous, but to a certain extent, I think you come to expect it actually—sad as it is," Julie said. "It still bothers me when someone dies without a family to care about them. I know there are reasons for it, and a lot of the time, there are good reasons, but that never gets easier for me. Everyone starts life with so much promise. It's hard for me to see people who end up with no one in their life. Everyone should matter to someone, I feel."

"The same thing was on my mind the other day. Carl was important to the community, and he changed a lot of lives here. He lived here a very long time, I want people to celebrate him, I want his life to mean something, as you said. It mattered, I know, but I want Carl the person, not the realtor, not the lighthouse keeper, just Carl, to have mattered to us," I said.

At that moment, it was clear that once this was all over, once we knew who was responsible, we would be pulled together to celebrate Carl and all the ways he touched Mongin Island. In this small community with its own challenges, we couldn't afford to get lost in the transactions of life.

Julie nodded. "That sure would be nice. I have no idea what his sister plans to do. But, there's time for all that after we find out what happened to him. So, tell me about your day."

"I will," I said. "But give me one moment." I took Buddy out to the side yard. As Buddy sniffed around for his spot, I closed my eyes and took a deep breath of island air. From somewhere in the back of my mind, I heard "take deep cleansing breaths," like a leftover mantra from a yoga class. This fresh, salty air pushed out the distractions and with one last centering breath, I was fortified. I took Buddy back inside, checked on my customers, grabbed my canvas tote from behind the counter, and popped back into the office.

Julie listened attentively as I walked her through my conversation with Parker Turner and his uncooperative response. "Kind of a weird reaction," Julie said. "I mean, well within his rights of course, but an odd reaction. Why put up an unnecessary roadblock? To buy time? We can get the court order if that's how he wants to play."

"Well, let's explore Amelia Burke first," I said and quickly brought her up to speed on this possible connection. Then, I shifted to the items we collected at Governor's Point. As I spoke, I pulled the plastic bags from my tote and told her how we had tried to carefully collect the evidence. Julie's excitement rose and I felt like someone on a drop-tower ride at the county fair as I watched it all unfold on her face.

"Thanks, Carr. I will log these into evidence." She placed the bags into the accordion folder she had on her lap and wrapped her fingers around its top corners.

I was too excited for that. "Tell what you're thinking," I demanded.

She began slowly, "I am not saying these aren't important, of course, you never know what matters in a case—but I don't want you to get your hopes up that these trinkets, which could have been left there by anyone at any time, will be impactful. That's all, that's all I am saying."

I surprised myself at how defensive I felt, like I had just taken a gut punch. Then, I realized that I knew this feeling. I had always hated producing work that wasn't excellent. I spoke slowly, trying to hide my disappointment, "You don't know that these things aren't important. I know I have seen that anchor before. I just can't remember where. It will come to me."

"Well, when you remember more, tell me," Julie said.

"Before we move on—Scott Campino does not know anything specific about Evan Weisman. He is familiar with the name as a real estate investor and a developer but really, that's about it. I guess the big reveal would have been Saturday, when they were all together."

"That makes total sense. We spoke to Mr. Weisman. He was supposed to travel to Mongin on Friday night and stay at the Inn. He confirmed that he was supposed to meet Carl for breakfast on

Saturday and then head over to Governor's Point. But, Mr. Weisman said that his office called the Inn and canceled his reservation on Thursday morning due to an unexpected commitment he needed to attend to. He sent along the cancellation email, the screen shot of the phone call, and documentation of his travel to Colorado Springs. He was not even on the east coast—he is not involved in this—except to say he was considering Governor's Point as an investment."

"So, you've confirmed that he was the mystery investor Carl was talking to."

"Not just talking, I guess they had met several times. Carl toured some of his other properties and they had some meetings with his finance people. According to Mr. Weisman, they spent some time together—getting to know each other—and Carl did quite a bit of due diligence. This could have been a massive project for Carl—not only the land but eventually new homes sold to future owners. Big, big money. Mr. Weisman has an alibi, as I said, but we are still looking into the information regarding the deal."

"And, one more thing," she added. "He called Carl several times and emailed him, never heard back. Both on Thursday and on Friday. Now he knows why. I broke the news to him and have to say the man was definitely stunned. Mr. Weisman is not a man who is usually ignored and he did not appreciate the lack of response. Of course, this was before he knew what had happened. Unfortunately for Scott Campino, I think it's going to be hard to get Mr. Weisman reinterested in a project here again." Julie sat back and rubbed her hands on her thighs. She was beginning to show signs of strain too.

Clearing her throat, she said, "Let's just see where all this takes us. We will process this evidence and see what we can find out about Amelia Burke. Now, let me tell you about what we found on Beach Road before I catch the boat back to the mainland."

She looked at her watch and spoke quickly. Her story began with their exploration of the lot on Beach Road and she listed all the things her team collected as she scanned her notebook. "This is probably the most immediately usable piece of information, I guess you could call it a clue, that we found today. So, for the purposes of discussion, let's agree that Carl Tibbons was hit in the head, maybe by a good-sized rock, okay? And also let's agree that the large pool of blood next to the trampled grass is Carl's. It is being tested right now to confirm this, but for now, let's just walk through the situation." She looked up to see if I was following this.

"Alright, so Carl Tibbons passed away at the lot on Beach Road, Thursday morning. How did he end up at Governor's Point?" Julie asked me like it was the first time anyone had thought of it.

"Julie, that's what we have been wondering since we first found out Carl did not drown! I mean, that's the million-dollar question we have all asked!" I said.

"Right! But it is an especially pertinent question when you consider we pulled only ten-inch tire tracks out of the clearing path on the Beach Road lot. We have other sets of tracks going into the clearing and those are the standard eight-and-a-half inches. So, we had someone with a regular cart drive into the site, right? But, someone with a bigger, non-standard cart drove both in and out. And more importantly, both of those tire sizes are too narrow for a gas-powered car or truck, so we are only looking for carts."

I gasped. "You mean someone *did* drive across the island and through the woods with Carl Tibbons, who was already dead or at least actively dying, in a golf cart? An open-air golf cart? This is what you're saying? How did this happen without anyone seeing it?"

"The way I see it, it must have been pretty early on Thursday morning," Julie said. "Carl must have met someone at Beach Road. Some kind of altercation occurred and Carl was seriously injured. We know he did not die immediately. Eventually, he was loaded into someone's cart and his own cart was moved—and somehow wound up going down that embankment, where the land drops off. My thinking is that someone drove their own cart to Governor's Point, so they could then get home or maybe to the dock to get off the island. We've got the ferry passenger lists for that day and everyone on it is accounted for. So, at the end of it, we come to this: Whoever caused Carl's death either left on some other boat we haven't identified—or is likely still on the island."

I absorbed all this, then said, "Maybe we should consider the possibility that Carl was able to be seated in the cart and driven to Governor's Point. If that happened, maybe the killer waited with him out there near the pool, watched him suffer, and then ultimately pass away. What a cruel and heartless thing to do!"

"The trouble with an injury like Carl's is that oftentimes a person may not know they have a brain bleed and if they don't get medical treatment, they die," Julie said. "In this case, if we had a chance to examine him after he had been hit, the cut on his head and the bruising would have been a good indication of something else going on, but, of course, we didn't get that chance. I'm saying, if someone had seen him, or found him, this could have been a preventable death."

The idea of such a missed opportunity was a very heavy thought. Julie was right, there was a lot to process. "Somehow, it feels like we let Carl down," I said sadly. "Logically, I know this isn't exactly the case, I haven't actually heard that someone saw him and did nothing to help. I guess it's just the magnitude of what could have been done to save him."

"Indeed, yes," she said. "So many times, people find themselves victims of terrible circumstances. But—I guess that's all I can tell you now. I am sorry to say, the sheriff's boat is waiting for me. I am going to head out now. Let's talk tomorrow morning. Hopefully, I will have a few things back from the labs and I can give you an update."

As we walked together to the front porch, I realized that the customer who had been browsing a few minutes ago had left the store. "I am officially the worst shopkeeper," I said. "I completely ignored that person! I have to get it together."

Julie smiled kindly, "You can only do so many things at once. And, right now, you're busy solving crimes!"

"I should be busy running this store! But I am happy about the progress we made today. I feel like we just have to tie all these strings together."

As she climbed into the Tahoe, I yelled, "Julie, Julie, wait!" I waved my arms, hoping she would notice me as she backed up. She rolled down the window and leaned out.

"I remember where I saw that anchor charm, the one we found at Governor's Point. I can't believe it," I said. "That charm was on Missy's key ring, the one she had when she let me back into Carl's house on Sunday. That charm was on her key ring, I know it. She had to fiddle with the lock and the charm swung from side to side. I am certain of it."

We looked at each other but said nothing for a minute. Then, Julie said, "Well, that *is* interesting. Missy continues to be an enigma, that's for sure. Didn't she ask you why anyone would go to Governor's Point? At least we know she went there after Carl was found, after Carl was already dead. Right? You saw it on Sunday, so that means she went there later that day, or I guess some other day this week. The question is why. Why did she go to Governor's Point? What was she looking for? That is assuming this charm is hers, and not just a trinket from the lighthouse gift shop that anyone could have bought."

"I will swing by her house again tomorrow and ask her to show me Carl's wall map one more time so I can see her key ring," I said. "But I agree, now that we know it probably places her there after Carl died, it's probably a lower priority. That still leaves the silver piece we found, though."

We said goodbye, again, and she pulled quickly out of the parking lot, heading down Old Port Passage Way. It only took a minute to gather my things and lock up. Buddy and I were soon heading home.

Chapter 23

Lunch was a distant memory, so I was eager to eat as I pulled into my driveway. However, dinner was to be more utilitarian than any grand exercise in creating a culinary delight. It was hard to believe all that had happened today. After eating quickly, Buddy and I decided a quick walk would do us both a world of good. There weren't many people on the resort property yet. The tourist season was still several weeks from beginning. The Inn was all lit up. From the road, I could see the huge chandelier through the second story window. The warm glow guided my way till I was almost at the path to Barb's house. I decided against an impromptu visit, feeling like my head was already filled with so much noise, I wouldn't be much company tonight.

As we approached the Beach Club restaurant, I noticed a few familiar faces gathered near the parked carts. "Hi, friends, it's great to see y'all," I called out as we all smiled and waved. I could feel them willing me to stop to chat—but I decided against that.

Back at home, showered and refreshed, my curiosity could no longer be contained. Who was Amelia Burke and what was her connection to the land on Mongin Island that would lead to such a substantial investment? Over the years, it was one of the things that surprised us most about this island. To someone who didn't know better, it would seem relatively few people had invested in Mongin Island. Proportioned to the number of available home sites, there weren't many actual homes. You could drive down some roads, even on the resort property, and see only one or two houses. This could give the impression people didn't invest financially, emotionally, or physically here.

The county property maps told a vastly different story. Almost all of the lots on the resort property and much of the land down the dirt roads or in other neighborhoods belonged to someone. People do invest in Mongin Island, some more quietly, with a piece of land they hold onto until they are ready to take that next step. There is a common thread to many of our stories of how we got to Mongin Island. It was not surprising to hear someone tell a version of my own story. Someone came to visit and before they knew it, island magic was wrapped around that person. I was curious to know Amelia's story.

Almost two hours clicked by before my work yielded enough information to put together a tentative profile of this Amelia Burke. She was a middle-aged woman who used to live in San Diego, California, but currently lived in the United Kingdom. I thought she might be a British national and had spent only a few years in this country. The Beach Road parcel was purchased sixteen years ago, near the height of development on the island. Taxes have been paid on time, every year. Amelia Burke, the woman behind Mr. Parker Taylor's LLC, was diligent and she had been holding onto this property for a long time. Why did she now want to swap it for Governor's Point? Why not just list it and sell it?

The only way I could think to contact her was to reach out through different social media platforms and unfortunately wait for her response. Maybe Julie would be able to use more official channels to reach her. I put this on my growing "talk to Julie about this" list.

I rambled around the house, shifting knick knacks on the coffee and end tables, wiping down the shelves in the refrigerator, and folding and refolding the throw on the back of the sofa. Something felt like it was right there, right in front of me, but I couldn't put my finger on it. It was all hazy, right on the edge of understanding—when all of sudden, a chill went through me and the hairs on my arms stood up.

I knew this thought was significant in a way I couldn't fully understand yet. I knew where I had seen that silver piece we found today!

Chapter 24

There were several off-putting things about Paul Easton. He was demanding and self-centered, wrapped in a blanket of entitlement. All of this was true, at least to me. Normally, I am not overly interested in what other people wear or how they present themselves. However, I do notice the outliers who dress in ways that draw attention to themselves. Not because I want people to conform to some unwritten social norm, but because people who seek attention in this way intrigue me. It wasn't that he was better dressed than most of us, either. There were plenty of well-turned-out islanders and visitors.

Rather, Paul's manner of dress felt like a shield, blocking you from getting emotionally close to him—as if he had donned a costume to play a role. That fit with his stilted, formal, regulated speech. Time with Paul was time spent trying to figure out what he was really saying and thinking. He was, I thought, someone who remained completely unfamiliar, no matter how many times you were in his company. Trying to figure out Paul Easton made you focus on his words, his actions, and for me, even his clothes, and that's where I knew I had seen the silver oval before. It was a concho from Paul's belt, the belt Paul wore when he visited the store.

Now I remembered that belt clearly.

But could I prove that it was Paul's concho? Living in a golf community, concho belts were somewhat common, both on and off the course. Could I be sure this concho belonged to Paul? I looked closely at the evidence pictures I took before handing my plastic bags over to Julie. It was very likely that the letters and clubs engraved on this disk were tied to a golf club. If this was true, then this concho was likely from a belt purchased at that club pro shop. Could I find this specific club logo online?

"Ah-ha!" I shouted just a few minutes later, startling Buddy out of his deep sleep. A reverse-image search of the concho's face turned up Ganton Golf Club in England. The market for Ganton Golf Club belts on this small island four thousand miles away must be microscopic.

Still, for this to be solid evidence, I had to prove this concho came from a belt that belonged to Paul. I would definitely be visiting him in the morning, that was a given. Julie's skepticism over Missy's charm showed me I would need this proof, and that I'd get bonus points for proving it was there when we found Carl. With the time zone difference, the Ganton Club's pro shop and club desk would open in only a few hours. I would call to see if anyone knew Paul Easton.

If I made that connection, that would help with part one. Part two was a bit more challenging. How would I ever prove when this concho was left at Governor's Point? All the pictures I took on Saturday had been downloaded to my computer in order to share them with Julie. I turned on the television mounted above my stone fireplace in the family room and used AirPlay to review them on the large screen. I was surprised at how many shots I took that morning. I hardly remembered taking some of them and, at the time, my mind had not absorbed all the details I could now see.

I clicked quickly through more than a dozen photos because I wanted to get to the ones of the walkway where we found the concho. There was a series of fourteen shots of this general area taken in rapid succession. In the background, the first responders, detectives, and other professionals were visible as they worked the scene. In the foreground, I focused on the trampled grasses, the scuffed stones, and the gravel pushed to the sides of the path. There, in the top left corner of the screen, right where we paused to look at Barb's leg, was a ground-covering plant that looked like it had been trampled, and right below its variegated leaves, I could see a sliver of silver. I jumped from my chair, balancing my laptop on my left palm and using my right to zoom in on the image. Without blurring the screen, you could only see this hint of silver. Would this be enough? Could this prove that Paul had been at Governor's Point before we found Carl?

My adrenaline was pumping, but I was in a holding pattern for now. I couldn't speak to Paul and I couldn't contact the golf club yet. Restless to keep going, I searched my notes for any other avenue of research into Paul's life I could pursue at this hour—and I remembered his books! I dug into the box of books Bob Harkins brought over to me—to which I had added the less-expensive book he had found for Paul and mailed to me. I hadn't touched Bob's books because they reminded me of my own professional lapse with Bob and Monica. As a result, I wanted to wait until my mind had cleared and I could review these books carefully to provide meaningful feedback to Bob. I wanted to regain some credibility with him.

The little shelf of regional authors was proving quite popular with my customers—they had definitely embraced the idea of shopping locally. Bob's experience made me feel like I should just defer to his recommendations. I didn't have many of my own suggestions. Maybe I could have just accepted his guidance if I hadn't already felt so unimpressed by my own performance at Books & Brew this week. With this in mind, I settled down to review Bob's suggestions as thoughtfully and intentionally as I could.

The book he sent in the mail for Paul was the thickest one in the box—a book about treasure hunting in this region. It was divided into chapters based on location and included descriptions of each of these adventures, with an index that allowed readers to search for the type of treasure, location, and date the treasure was lost or found. The map printed inside the front cover was a nice touch. But why was this book on Paul's list? Suddenly, I spotted the extensive index of Mongin citations—and this book had my full attention. There were over a hundred pages about one Mongin story alone. When I learned that the treasure hunters were a team from the University of Georgia, I was hooked! Many of my old neighbors and their children attended UGA and I always had a soft spot for their bulldog mascot.

I dove into those pages! The UGA team, led in tandem by the chair of the southern studies program and a visiting adjunct professor, came to Mongin Island decades ago. Their charge was to find the missing graves belonging to an elite British army team ambushed by Native Americans in the battles that preceded the American Revolutionary War. It was rumored that gold and personal artifacts given by King George I were also buried with these troops. Depending on their final resting place, many people long believed these graves and treasures had washed out to sea decades ago as the island flooded, the water tables shifted, and various hurricanes hit Mongin Island. However, this UGA team had done extensive research and received the funding to look inland. There were several dig sites identified and the State Historic Preservation Office had issued permits allowing excavation.

It certainly was an intriguing story and I loved the black-and-white photograph of the explorers inserted after the first thirty pages. Seeing these pictures made me sentimental. Pictures from this time period helped me imagine what my dad must have looked like when he was a young man. My father died when I was a child, and I don't have many pictures of him. These men were dressed in the same dress code he probably would have selected: short-sleeved shirts tucked into khaki pants and dark ties. This made them seem familiar to me. Some wore dark-framed browline glasses, but all had short-cropped haircuts. They faced the camera hopefully. Their youthful confidence was easy to see.

The dig sites had been identified on a smaller map on the left side of the text and I noticed immediately they were all in the center and northwestern parts of the island. Much of Mongin was undeveloped when this research team was here years ago. To this day, many people still find Native American artifacts on the island, so I can only imagine the things that were unearthed fifty years ago.

Their story took me through the anticipation, exploration, and excavation process. As I read, I rode the highs and lows with the team. Reading between the lines, I sensed their dissatisfaction and urgency. There were several references to "tight deadlines" and long days of work that continued by flashlight some evenings. After a physically grueling two months and multiple sites explored, the British troops, if buried here, had not been found.

I felt a tug in my heart, looking at the pictures from the conclusion of the dig. The team looked stoically at the camera. Their exuberance and confidence were gone. Instead, exhaustion and disappointment replaced their previous joy. However, when I turned to the last page and saw the final group shot, it was the visiting professor's expression that was truly compelling and riveting. His heartbreak was so palpable, so real, looking at his photo made you want to reach out and pat his arm encouragingly, reassuring him that life would go on.

"All is now lost" was the quote attributed to Dr. Edward Easton on the last page.

Chapter 25

"It can't be. That is just not possible," I said, breaking the silence of my house.

Stunned was an understatement. There probably are words, somewhere in the world, to describe what I felt at that moment. But even now, I can't find them.

I read the name in the photo's caption again. My mind was thrown into reverse, forcing me to look at those words again and again. This was not a coincidence. This period in British history on pre-American soil, these urgent demands for information, the focus on this area, and how all these things fit together—this had to be Paul's father.

Even on that warm April night, I was chilled. I must have done ten or more laps from the kitchen through the family room into the dining room and study and back around, rubbing my crossed arms to warm myself up. Why were the Eastons so interested in this land—and the secrets it concealed? What was their connection here?

Fortunately, I realized it was now after 8 a.m. in England. Time to call the Ganton Golf Club. My initial excitement about this opportunity was long gone. The enormity of the day finally caught up to me. I stepped onto my screened porch and looked at the beautiful, clear night sky. There must have been a million stars in the sky, and the moon was bright. The night would be over soon. It was already tomorrow and I was just waiting for the sun to catch up.

Today would be another challenging day. It would start with a call to Julie to talk about the Eastons and to hear updates on the evidence she collected at Beach Road. Then, we would need to speak with Paul and we needed to strategize for that. There were so many questions—about Paul's books, his concho, and his family. And, what if we heard back from Amelia Burke? What if we didn't? I would need to try to find her as well. Did Theresa know Amelia Burke? Then, of course, there was Missy. What had she been doing at Governor's Point? Today already felt like I was sorting a brand new 500-piece jigsaw puzzle. Piece by piece, I could start building the puzzle's frame, but the main scene, the part inside the frame, was missing.

There was one last thing to do before I tried to grab at least a couple of hours of sleep! I placed the call to the Ganton Club pro shop. After several rings, a deep, male voice shouted a greeting: "Ganton Shop, Wesley here, will you be needing a tee time?"

It was surprisingly more casual than their website presented. From what I read, it was a club steeped in championships, history, and tradition, and to me, that meant a formality. "Hi Wesley, no thank you, I don't need a tee time, but I was wondering if you could help me?" I found myself shouting back at him. There was so much background noise, it was hard to hear.

"What can we do for you?" he said helpfully, and the noise subsided. I appreciated that he must have moved to an area outside the hub.

"I am calling regarding a belt a neighbor of mine has—a belt from your club, I believe. I can tell by the insignia on its silver pieces." I tried to sound more confident than I felt. As I said the words out loud, I had second thoughts. Self-doubt, so familiar these days, appeared firmly at my side. Golf clubs on a golf belt? How many logos have these in them? There must be dozens of clubs, maybe hundreds of clubs with the initials G and C in their name. All of this was clearer to me a few hours ago.

He answered, "Right, our leather concho. You're talking about the standard course belt, or our deluxe championship model? Would you mind holding a bit? I am here alone and we have several members ready to head out. Be back in a flash, luv."

Before I could answer, I was listening to Vivaldi's Four Seasons, Spring, as I held the line. A few minutes passed and Wesley was back. "Right, sorry to delay, which style were you calling about?"

"While I was holding, I looked at the merchandise on your website. I am afraid I don't know the model but I found that it was your club from the logo on the concho and I ..."

Wesley jumped in: "Logo? The golf clubs and G and C? Not the Ganton gorse flower?

"Right, the clubs and the initials, not a flower," I said.

He chuckled and said, "Okay, well, you have yourself a standard model then, luv. What can we do for you?"

Here comes the story, I thought, and said, "Well, unfortunately, my neighbor lost one of the conchos, popped right off it seems, while he was doing some outside work. I would like to replace the belt for him, knowing how much he loves it. I was wondering if you could help me figure out which one to get him."

He didn't answer immediately. I heard the register chiming and another phone line ringing but finally, he said. "Well now, that's quite a bugger, isn't it? Next to our navy jumpers, these belts fly out of this store. In all my days, I do not recall anyone losing a concho. It is what our members and their guests expect and pay for. I assure you, our vendors are the best you will find. We don't offer inferior products, I can tell you that."

Somehow my inquiry seemed to have offended him and now we were off track. "Would you be able to help me replace the one my neighbor has? I know it would mean the world to him," I said, hoping this would appeal to his sentimental side, assuming he had one. "I don't have all the information you need like his size, but I was hopeful you could maybe search your sales records to see what he bought. I wanted this to be a surprise for him, of course."

Reluctantly, at least that was what I interpreted his slowed response to mean, he agreed and said that if I provided the member or guest name, he would be able to search records from the last three years, assuming my neighbor charged his club account or used a credit card. Three years ago, the club had installed a new payment system, so those were the only accessible records. We exchanged contact information. I provided Paul's name to Wesley. If Paul was a member, Wesley had no reaction.

"Hmmm, luv, I'm not finding an entry here in our system, but I can do a little more digging in our records."

In a moment of what can only be described as divine intervention or some other supernatural inspiration, I blurted out: "Wesley, before we hang up—perhaps Ms. Amelia Burke purchased this for Paul Easton?" I held my breath and noticed both hands were clenched into tight balls.

He replied instantly, with a whole new different tone. Gone was the offended, reluctant Wesley. He was oddly deferential. "Why, of course, apologies for not connecting Mr. Easton to Ms. Burke. Of course, now that you say it. Apologies, certainly, luv. I didn't realize we were speaking of this specific Mr. Easton. It is entirely my fault. Because you were talking about a neighbor, I assumed it was an American guest playing here. Yes, of course, please extend my apologies to Mr. Easton and Ms. Burke. If I remember right, this was already a replacement belt, as he needed a different size. We haven't seen Mr. Easton in several weeks, but Ms. Burke is a great patron of our club and has done wonders for the ladies' program. Were you in attendance at their anniversary party we hosted? Lovely, lovely night, incredibly generous for them to have included the entire club. Wonderful, wonderful event."

When he finally stopped talking, I suggested he email me his findings. He assured me he would and from the tone of his voice, I knew this was one promise he would keep. As the call disconnected, I collapsed into an overstuffed chair. This day was just beginning, and it started with perhaps the biggest bombshell yet.

Amelia Burke, the landowner on Beach Road, was married to Paul Easton.

Chapter 26

I didn't expect to sleep. I thought I was going to spend a few hours staring at the tray ceiling above my bed, replaying all the scenes, conversations, and open-ended issues. Instead, I worked out a plan for beginning my day, and then, somehow, I fell asleep. When the alarm chimed, I jumped, startled from the deepest sleep I had in days, disoriented that these few hours had passed so quickly.

While still in bed, wrapped protectively in my smooth sheets and soft comforter, I knew I had to reach out to Julie. We traded several texts, one right after the other. She and her team would arrive at my house in about one hour and we would talk in person. There was so much to share. We didn't say what we each had found in the hours we spent working, but she said her time had been very productive.

I promised, "And, wait until you hear what I found!"

Slowly, almost painfully, I moved from the bed and started to get ready. The lack of sleep, the adrenaline, the weight of the discoveries, and reality were weighing on me. I felt burdened, achy, and foggy. Buddy, bless his heart, must have sensed something was way off, because he kept me in his line of sight. He watched protectively, following me to all the rooms I moved through. His concern touched me and I went to reassure him. Rubbing that special spot under his left ear and the white fluff on his chest, we restarted our day in a much better way. He gently licked my face and nestled his little head into my neck. We would be okay, together.

"Let's get breakfast ready. Are you hungry, little boy?" I asked him cheerfully. Buddy had worked his own version of Mongin Island magic. I prepped some coffee, made a big batch of pancakes, and filled a plate with a pile of bacon while I waited for Julie's team to arrive. If this day was going to go as I anticipated, we would probably be sitting here together for some time. While things were cooking, I called Tripp to confirm he would be able to watch the store—yet again.

"I am sensing last night was successful for you, Carr?" he asked.

"Tripp, yes, without a doubt. Julie is on her way over and I think we will be in a much different place by tomorrow. That's all I am saying for now," I said. "Thank you so much for holding down the fort, once again."

"No worries at all, Carr, not a problem. My house is being power washed. I would rather be at the store than smell bleach and listen to the water on the siding all day. Do you want to bring Buddy by? He can keep me company if you want. You know, funny thing, I was thinking we may want to add him to the store's webpage. People are asking about him. He has quite the following around here."

"Tripp, great idea, I love it. Maybe that will encourage some of the children to stop in, too. If you wouldn't mind, I think Buddy enjoys being with all the people, rather than sitting alone in this house. Let's plan on it, but if we can't get there, I will text you. I am not exactly sure what is going to happen today or what the schedule will be, to be honest." I said, once again offering up a silent prayer of thanksgiving for Tripp.

Next call was to Barb. "You will not believe all that has happened. Julie is on her way over to my house. Can you come too?" I blurted out as soon as she answered.

"I'm on my way," she said without asking any other questions. Hearing her voice made me immediately calm. I called and she came—no questions asked, no formality, no explanation needed. Just a friend, a true friend, showing up. We were perfectly imperfect people but we knew what mattered and we made sure we each knew what that was. She would be here to support me, she knew I thought I needed her strength, and she would give it to me. It was as simple and as pure as that.

Barb got there first. She knocked and walked in. "Carr, you look exhausted. Have you slept at all?" Her face showed her concern.

"A little, not much, to be honest," I said as I fixed her coffee and started another pot. "Barb, look, before everyone gets here, I want to tell you how much I appreciate you, all you have done, you tolerating my crazy, half-baked ideas. I am not sure where we are heading, but I think we are close to the finish line. I just want you to know, I want you to hear how much I appreciate you."

She didn't say anything at first but then she smiled and said, "Thank you, Carr. I thought you may have been a smidge angry or maybe disappointed that I wasn't as fearless as you are. I have a feeling your impact on Mongin Island is just beginning and I am, honestly, glad to be part of it. I think Tripp is right, I think you are a softy."

As I finished getting ready, I heard the cars pull up. Voices soon filled my kitchen. Barb was getting everyone started on breakfast and coffee. I took one last look in the mirror and gave myself a brief pep talk. "We have come this far. We need to push a little more to get across the finish line." With that, I shut off the light and joined the team.

Every available surface in my kitchen and screened porch now was covered with some kind of laptop, printer, or other device. Every outlet had multiple plugs stuffed into it and there were surge protectors draped across the floor like criss-crossed roads. People were eating, talking, and busy setting up, but that came to halt when Julie stood up and asked for everyone's attention.

"Team, I know we have a lot to cover and a lot to report. I asked Cole to document our time together this morning. He will keep a running tally of all we discuss and will be creating this live document to share on the whiteboard. Cole, is the whiteboard ready to go?" she asked. Cole was setting up some kind of integrated technology that let his computer display what he typed on the board.

"It will be, one more minute. We are having trouble with the encryption on this network, but we are about there," Cole said, fiddling with the cords behind the portable board.

Julie continued, "Excellent. Here is how I want to do this. I will start, then I want the group with the forensic and pathology reports to chime in. After that, let's hear from those who worked with witnesses, and I think your group included some financial analysis, right? Last and certainly not least, Carr can tell us what she learned, and then we should have a good go-forward strategy. Everybody ready?"

I made eye contact with Barb, who was leaning over my kitchen island. She winked and gave me a thumbs-up, which seemed wonderfully ridiculous given the gravity of our discussion. I loved it, she knew exactly what I needed. Our session began and continued for at least one hour before it was my turn to speak. While I waited my turn, I listened to the reports and the numerous specific details we had collected. I was in awe of how much work had been done by this entire team. In just a few days, we had pieced together an almost complete picture of Carl and the people who rotated around him in his world. The sheer volume of information was beyond impressive. Cole's list, displayed on the screen set up in front of my fireplace, was scrolling from page to page as he typed quickly. When it was finally my turn, I took a deep breath and began our story, starting from finding the cart over the embankment at the Beach Road property and finishing twenty minutes later with the introduction of Dr. Edward Easton, who, like his son, was captivated, perhaps obsessed, with Mongin Island.

I spoke in almost a trance, entirely focused on relaying the facts in the same sequence I discovered them. My goal was to present the evidence to the professionals so they would direct the next step. Near the end of my contribution, I looked up from my notes and found the faces of the team gathered here, in my home. While I had been reading and speaking, I had not noticed the intensity of the team or the way their eyes were glued to me. People were literally on the edges of their chairs. The room was completely silent, except for Cole's typing.

Finally, Julie stood up and walked over to the doors out to my porch. With her back to our group, she said, ever so quietly, "My God, Carr, you did it, you solved the case."

Chapter 27

The room erupted in cheers and clapping. It was incredibly emotional to see how invested this team was in finding out what happened and how much they wanted to speak for the victim of the crime, who no longer had a voice. This was the way "it" was supposed to work. It was the golden rule and the idea of karma, of putting things out into the world that you wouldn't mind getting back. It was a moment I hoped I would never forget.

"What? No, I didn't," I said, "Julie no, that's very flattering, but I just did what you asked. I spoke to people and got them to tell me things."

I felt my cheeks burning and looked for Barb in the crowd of people standing in the room. Barb was still in front of the island and had her hands on either side of her nose, covering her mouth. Her eyes were shining with what I thought could have been tears, although she likely would have never admitted it to me or anyone else. Catching my eye, she dropped her hands and gave me another thumbs-up, which made me chuckle. Someone started to gather the plates and mugs and someone else was loading my dishwasher. I wanted that magical moment back. I didn't want the spell to be broken.

I said, "Wait, everyone, we still need to find out more about Dr. Easton and tie it all together, right? I don't think we are done yet."

"No, of course, we aren't done yet, but we are dang close," Julie said. From the back corner, one of Julie's officers said, "I have something, Cole. Can you stop sharing your screen for a minute and let me share this?" It took a few minutes of connecting and clicking, but then we were ready to go.

The screen filled with database searches and articles from different sources. We all read quickly and quietly. Julie corralled the group after we processed several articles. "Okay, team, so I think we have enough to get a general idea of how to move forward." She stood at the kitchen island and outlined her plan. Immediately, people sprang into action, breaking down the technology, updating files, and preparing for the afternoon in front of us. Several officers would be heading back to the mainland office to work on further research, but a core group would stay behind. My heart was pounding as I listened to our next steps.

Reality was here. We had left the theoretical, the puzzle of it all.

Julie said, "Carr, I want you to reach out to Paul and see if he will meet you someplace with some element of privacy. I guess we can go to his rental, but that won't give us the chance to set up a video recording and it would be weird to invite him to your house. I won't ask that of you. What I want is a place he can be interviewed. Remember—this is not an interrogation. If all goes according to plan, that will happen on the mainland. We'll need to talk to Missy, too."

"How about if I close Books & Brew for the afternoon?" I offered. "It would only be for a few hours and I can offer a special something for people who are inconvenienced. Let me reach out to Tripp now and then I will call Paul for his availability. He wanted to talk to me yesterday, but I didn't get to him. I think I can get him to meet me someplace, but it may be tough. He doesn't do anything he doesn't want to do. Do we have a Plan B if I can't convince him?"

Julie smiled, "You can be sure of that, Carr, you can be so sure of that. He won't like our Plan B any more than he will like you telling him his needle in the haystack books can't be found yet."

After a few calls, it was arranged. Missy agreed, though she sounded suspicious on the phone. Tripp asked no questions and offered to take care of the communication plan for our customers. He indicated we had a busy morning so far but things were starting to slow down. It was no surprise on such a beautiful beach day. Many people would want to take advantage of the mild spring weather. The store would be empty by 1 p.m.

Paul, on the other hand, wasn't as easy, of course. The conversation began with a dissertation on all the ways we had disappointed him. Without having made the progress on his request he expected, Paul was not interested in meeting me in person. I told him that I had received one book that was on his list, which I could give him if he stopped by the store. He demanded to know which book it was. When I told him, he made it clear it was not the book he was most eager to find. Although he was doubtful, angry, frustrated, and who knows what else, he finally agreed. Dealing with him on other occasions was a challenge, but today was next level. Maybe I was sensitive this time because I knew what was in front of us. Or maybe he was just becoming unhinged. It was hard to tell. The most important thing was—this was happening. We just needed to get all the players in place. A few more calls and we would be done.

The team headed to the store. Barb, Buddy, and I went first in my golf cart. This gave us time to do some preliminary setup and explain the plan to Tripp. "You said you would be willing to help us, right? This may be way out of your comfort zone. I understand that and I want to give you a few minutes to think through this before Julie gets here. You don't have to do this, there is no pressure, Tripp," I said as gently as I could.

"No, Carr, I want to do this. I want to be here with y'all and help in some small way. Just tell me what I need to do," Tripp said, his arms wrapped protectively around his middle.

We locked eyes and I was trying to see what he wasn't saying. "Seriously, you don't have to do this."

He tilted his head slightly, "I think that is where you are wrong, Carr. I think I do need to do it. Can't hide behind grief and fear and disappointment forever, right? I should be part of the community. I have a responsibility to do what I know is right. You did it, right? You were uncomfortable and out of your element, but you did it. Just tell me what to do, and I will follow your lead."

Tripp had just finished speaking as Julie entered the room. She and I looked at each other as she stood at the store's threshold. She nodded slightly and turned to her team to get everyone in place. There wasn't much time and we needed to work quickly. "We good?" she asked.

I replied, probably sounding more confident than I felt, "Yes, we are all good, ready to go."

In a last-minute scramble, Julie and Cole were in my office with the door partially closed, for now. The two other officers had set up the video and recording equipment in the kitchenette. Tripp was stationed behind the register. From my seat at the Trading Floor table, I watched his lips move silently as he rehearsed the suggestions Julie had given him. Tripp was silently carrying out what looked like both sides of a potential dialogue, complete with hand gestures to make his point.

Chapter 28

The front door was locked, so when Missy arrived, Tripp had to walk across the store to let her in. If she was curious about the circumstances of this meeting, she did not show it. Tripp brought her to the table where Barb and I were seated, discussing the recent events. "Missy, hi, thanks for coming so quickly. This really shouldn't take long. Please, have a seat." I gestured to the chairs on Barb's side of the table. Interestingly, Buddy did not get out of his chair to greet her. For such a friendly dog, it was curious that he had no interest in seeing her, someone with whom he had spent considerable time.

She sat down in the closest chair and looked around the room. "It's nice in here. It looks so different now that all the T-shirt stuff is gone. It's a nice spot." She smiled as she spoke, but I got the first glimpse that she was uncomfortable. Her face was flushed and she pulled distractedly on a silver ring on her right hand. "What did you want to talk about?"

"Just a couple of things, really. The first, I guess, is Governor's Point. We are hoping you can help us, Missy. Just seems like we have a lot of inconsistent information, so I thought we would start at the beginning," Barb answered for me as I gathered my thoughts.

Missy's eyes went over my head and she saw the prints of the pictures I took last Saturday. In all the events, I hadn't had time to get them professionally printed and framed. Even at these small sizes, Missy recognized Governor's Point. Her expression revealed as much to me.

"You asked me why anyone would go there," I said, "So I guess it's time for me to ask you that same question. Why did you go there, Missy? What were you looking for?"

"I don't know what you are talking about, I—" she answered quickly, sitting straight up in her chair.

"Let's not do that Missy. We already know you were there, we just want to understand why. Why did you go? You said you knew nothing about the property or anything Carl was working on, so why would you go to Governor's Point sometime after last Saturday?"

Missy silently looked from me to Barb and then back to me. Finally, she said, "I went to see what everyone was talking about—and that's not a crime. I can do that if I want. I wanted to see, I just wanted to know, I guess—not that I owe you any kind of explanation." She paused and then continued, "And how did you know I was there? Did someone tell you that? I mean you can't prove I was there, not that you have to or anything."

"We found something that belongs to you, Missy, at Governor's Point. That's how we know. It is just odd for someone who has no connection there to go to a crime scene and not mention it," I answered her, not referencing the lighthouse charm specifically. Honestly, I wasn't sure how much to reveal. In the rush to get this all set up, we didn't cover every detail with Julie and her team. Right now, we were just making it up as we were going along. I still wasn't certain that particular charm belonged to her.

"Can I see your cart key and your key ring?" I asked.

Her head jerked back. "No, actually, I don't think you can." She crossed her arms in front of her chest.

Barb and I were looking at her, waiting for her to say something else. We were locked like this when I saw Tripp head back toward the door and we heard Paul enter the store. "I assume you may know why I am here, is that correct?" he asked Tripp, speaking in his usual clipped tone, as if Tripp was the household help, like his butler or something.

"That I do, yes, come through this way," Tripp said, even bowing slightly as he said it. He guided Paul with his left arm, who soon saw Missy sitting with us. And, there it was, just a glimpse of recognition. If you blinked, you would have missed it. It was that ever so slight flash of an exchange between them. I knew we were on the right path.

"So, Paul, this is Missy, I'm not sure if you two have met." I introduced them as Paul pulled a chair to the head of the table and sat down. Neither of them said a word.

Paul finally spoke first. "So, what supposed information do you now have for me? Your meaning is lost on me. And where is my book? It is my hope you are expeditious about this. As you well know, I am working on a very time-sensitive project."

"Well, I can see you have other things to talk about, I don't know anything about your books. I'll head out and—" Missy started to stand up.

Barb leaned forward, gently touched her arm, and said firmly, "We would really like for you to stay." Missy sat back down, but I wasn't sure how long she would comply. Barb turned to Paul almost at the same time and said, "Yes, Paul, we are all well aware." I think we had all reached the end of our patience with Paul. Barb did not even try to mask her annoyance with him. He shot her a menacing look but did not reply.

Everything that happened these past few days was coming down to this moment, this conversation. It was hard to believe a week ago our biggest concern was adding decor to this very room to make it feel more inviting, more like a home on Mongin Island. "It must begin so it can end," I said, more to myself than to anyone in particular.

"Paul—" I began, searching his face for some sign of recognition of what was coming. Seeing none, I was disappointed, but continued, "Paul, at your request, I contacted my book distributors and wholesalers, hoping they could find some of the volumes you requested. And, fortunately, a few were resourceful enough to use their networks, as you are aware."

Mirroring Missy, Paul sat back, crossed his arms, and almost shouted, "If this is your idea of an update, I must bid you good day!"

"Just listen! Will you *please* just stop talking?" Barb yelled at him, like she had been storing it up all week. Missy shifted away from her, putting distance between them.

I smiled slightly at Barb. The woman called it as she saw it. You had to give her that. Paul didn't even respond, his mouth open in slight shock.

I continued, "As you have reminded us, your obscure request has been a challenge, to say the least. Not that I haven't tried to help you but, yes, I have been unsuccessful. What has bothered me from the beginning was, why did you need these specific books for this mysterious research and project? I think I may understand that better now, no thanks to you, but let's pause on the why for now."

Grabbing my iced tea, I took a long sip, stretched a little in my seat, and then continued. "One of my book distributors was kind enough to drop off some potential new inventory selections, and he also sent me one of the books on your list."

"So, where is it?" Paul demanded, moving to the front of his chair, as if preparing to leave.

This time it was Tripp who appeared in the doorway and calmly but forcefully said, "Paul, we are not going to ask you again." The vagueness of this statement must have given him pause. Paul remained seated, silent. Missy alternated between looking at each of us, searching for a clue as to what was coming, and then staring at her lap. She had wrapped her arms around herself protectively.

"The book my colleague found for you is about treasure hunting," I said. "Specifically about a famous dig on Mongin Island. But unfortunately, these treasure hunters weren't successful. I think you might be interested in this, Paul, because these people were researching a lot of the same things in which you are interested. They were searching for graves of British soldiers killed in the pre-American Revolutionary

War period, right here on Mongin Island. Funny enough, that's what you were researching too, right Paul?"

Paul spoke through tight lips, barely moving. His words were like a hiss. "Yes, that is what interests me, I thought I made that absolutely clear to you, Carr. How tremendously disappointing that this simple concept was lost on you."

"Ahh yes, that old disappointment. Funny you mention that, actually, Paul. In this story, that was exactly what made an emotional connection to me as a reader. It was the disappointment the team felt at the end of their time on the island. There is a picture in the book that really helps you connect to this team of researchers. But the person who stood out the most was a professor who helped guide this team. His disappointment was so tangible and real, you almost felt it through the photo on the page. And, it turns out you share something else with this professor, Paul, something more than just your interest in events that occurred during this historical period." I paused, took a breath, and delivered the final blow. "Is Edward Easton your father? If he is, then I think we need to talk about the King's Cross."

Chapter 29

Missy gasped and yelled, "You didn't tell me this. Your father? What's your deal, Paul?"

"Shut up, you stupid woman! My father is no concern of yours," Paul snapped. "My deal? It is you who are unhinged, drawing unnecessary attention with your theatrics." He took a moment and smoothed his hair, tugged at his cuffs. He smiled at us in the most unfriendly way and said, "My father was a world-class lecturer who helped many people understand this period of time. That's all. He was an educator, and a highly regarded one, at that."

"That seems true," I said. "I am sure it is, but that still doesn't explain all that has gone on here this past week. Let me tell you what I think happened and then you can tell me where I am wrong, as I am sure you will. Okay, Paul? Missy, feel free to chime in, too. I imagine you have a very interesting perspective. I think you are very much like your father, Paul. You have been studying this area, researching it, and trying to get it right for a long time, which is why you visit here every year. You are trying to find these graves and treasures. It is vitally important for you to find these things, right? How am I doing? Am I right so far?"

"So the part that hasn't made sense to me, since the first time we spoke, is what was the urgency?" I continued. "What was so time-sensitive that fed this urgent request? It wasn't that your visit would be ending soon. Your rental is up in two weeks, so it wasn't that, right? I can't imagine that was it because you rent the same place for the same amount of time every year, and while I hear you have been demanding and ornery in the past, this urgency is over the top, even for you."

Julie told me to pause and wait in between these bold statements when we were rehearsing, but it was challenging to pace myself like this. I just wanted to race to the end and know how all the pieces fit into place. I began again, "It was your dad who helped me understand the urgency. 'All is now lost' was such an impactful, morose statement. It made me wonder about what he was referencing."

When Paul interrupted, it was with a voice I hadn't heard from him. Soulfully, he said, "You have no idea the depth of this loss. Do you know what it is like to live your life and always be an outsider? Do you know what it is like to never be accepted? This is the way our family hoped to earn the recognition we deserve. Generation after generation, serving the court, but never being part of it. This is the way—making this discovery after all these centuries—and then it would be done. We would be recognized and we would never be questioned again."

I left him with his thoughts for a few moments and tried to decide if I should bring Missy into this yet. She was silent, as if she was judging how much to reveal. I was still not absolutely sure about her role. I made the decision to continue with Paul. We were close.

"Exactly, Paul, that is how I understand it. So, let me see if we got it right. Centuries ago, King Henry VIII decreed that he would offer a solid gold cross to the man who served his king, his country, and the people in the 'noblest' of ways. Kind of a vague decree if you ask me, but of course, this gave him the leeway to award it as he wished and was in line with his vision that he would live forever.

"So, every fifty years, on the first day of June, the current monarch has the ability to award the King's Cross to a worthwhile recipient. And with this award comes the possibility the monarch will make this recipient a nobleman. In your case, you would go from a commoner to being appointed a viscount, which means you would formally enter royal ranks. This would happen in a formal, public ceremony. Right?

"June 1st is an important date in English royal history. From what I can tell, it is when Anne Boleyn was executed, which meant that Henry VIII felt he was liberated, elevated and, as legend goes, it is when he felt he could also elevate others who served him to the highest level. The monarch has kept this award on this date because, through time, other events happened on June 1st as well. It's considered an auspicious date.

"So Paul and Missy, this is where you come in. Paul, I believe you thought you finally had found the place the British troops were buried, at Governor's Point. Years ago, you thought it might be over by Beach Road, which is why you and your wife purchased that land. But that turned out to be a dead end, so you held onto that while you continued your search. Somehow you found out that the real spot is Governor's Point, but you needed access. I am guessing you had Missy work on Carl, maybe even push him to meet with you. Unfortunately, I don't think Carl saw the potential in the trade you suggested, especially since he had another prospect for a sale. When you met with Carl and he declined your offer, things took a turn, right Paul?"

Missy jumped in, "All I was supposed to do was to tell Carl about the deal and to introduce them. He did ask me to arrange the meeting at the Beach Road property, which I did, but that's it. I didn't know he killed him until you told me Carl was dead, I had no idea, I swear. I really did think Carl went off with Theresa to celebrate finally getting rid of that property after all these years."

I nodded but said nothing for a second, absorbing this information. "So, I guess that is what Carl meant by the green pin on his board. It wasn't a sold property, and it wasn't a current listing. The green marked a potential trade."

Missy shrugged her shoulders and replied, "I guess, yes, he didn't say. I thought Carl would have appreciated my being interested in his business and would like to work on deals together. So, when he still dumped me, even though I basically dropped this right into his lap and solved a problem for him, I just couldn't get past that. Theresa was that much better than me? Her deals were better than mine? I don't think so, but—"

Paul could take no more, "The book you were supposed to find—the eighteenth-century book—has the exact description of the land. I could report that we had finally found this historic site. We could eventually repatriate the remains, recover the artifacts. His Royal Highness would see it, he needed to see that book as proof that—then this would work, do you understand this? I needed the proof of the actual text—not my word, not the word of my father. In London, the council needs to see the physical book before the first of June. I have been searching for the site, for the books—for any proof, for years. Do you understand this? For years. You, and all those others, failed me."

He was nearly shouting. "But that Carl! That man would not see things clearly. All he kept saying was that Beach Road wasn't a good enough trade for Governor's Point, so he didn't feel it was in his client's best interest. Well, what about my best interest? What about me? What about my family? He was going to sell it! I know he was, and they would have built houses, and pour new foundations, and—and who knows what. I know he was! That man would not listen. He didn't care."

Paul kept pouring out his rage. "We have been part of the royal court for generations, bowing and scraping, but never made noble. Always serving, but never an equal, always thought of like the help. Returning these soldiers and the fortune buried with them is a great service and we should be rewarded. This is worthy of the King's Cross—others received it for far, far less, I can assure you. Carl wouldn't listen to any of it. The man was so infuriating that—yes, when things took an unexpected turn, I brought him to Governor's Point, thinking a new buyer surely wouldn't purchase this property, given this unfortunate event. I did not anticipate you two would have found him. Honestly, why did it have to be you, and not the other buyer Mr. Campino was pursuing?"

"Unfortunate event?" I said, my voice rising. "You killed someone!"

"He wasn't worth—" And that's when Julie and Cole appeared.

Julie read Paul and Missy their rights and they were handcuffed. As they were led out of the store, Paul turned to me and said, "My father was right, Carr—all is now lost."

Chapter 30

A few weeks later, on Memorial Day weekend, we gathered on the expansive back lawn of the Inn. It was a beautiful Saturday in May and Mongin Island was glowing. The sun was shining, the sea was sparkling, and the warm, gentle breeze moved the Spanish moss on the lower branches of the oaks, framing our group. We were there to honor Carl, to celebrate him, his life, and his contributions to our island. As we greeted each other, ate together, and spent time together, we were reminded that this island and our time on it was what gave us roots.

Mongin Island isn't for everyone, but it is for us. Our lives, even for those who came here alone by choice or by other circumstances, were entwined like the roots of trees that shade and protect us. Our neighbors, our community, our island, were part of each of us.

We heard that Carl's small family had opted for a short private service. They did not share the event details with us. We were not surprised. What did surprise us was how little we collectively knew about that family as we tried to piece together the things about Carl we never got to ask. In all the years Carl lived on the island, no one could recall any visits from his family. No one could clearly say who his biological family was, and through these discussions it was confirmed, when it came right down to it: we were his family. Although we weren't related by blood, we were tied together by the will to live independently, without many of the mainland conveniences. We were Carl's immediate and extended family. So today was our opportunity to gather to remember a man who had such an impact on us.

I was filled with a renewed energy and peace that only my family could provide. Meredith and Nicholas took a late ferry yesterday afternoon, which gave us plenty of time to catch up, walk on the beach, and play with Buddy. Anticipating their arrival had given me something to look forward to these past few weeks, but I couldn't relax until I saw them, listened to them, and felt their energy. This was the first time we would be in *La Vida Pacifica* without Rob. Sure, there were times in the past that we visited Mongin Island without him—but this time, there was no chance he would surprise us again, like he sometimes did, by walking through the door, humming a tune, and smiling as he said, "Do you think I would miss a chance to be with all my favorite people?"

It also concerned me that Carl's celebration of life would be the first memorial service we had all attended since Rob's. Would this be too painful? Is this all too much at one time? Once again, my children surprised me. Not by saying or doing anything extraordinary, but just by being their authentic selves. Rob's presence and the joy he brought to our lives was noticeably absent. But Meredith and Nicholas were healing and they were happy to have a chance to celebrate life. Having my children under my roof, having them in their beds, their shoes by the door, their bags on the floor, their voices traveling down the hall, them playing rock, paper, scissors to decide who would get to have Buddy keep them company last night—having their presence here in our home enabled me to sleep soundly. I woke up truly content.

Tripp, Barb, and I had arranged the details of this important event with the resort and left it open to all who wanted to join.

"What a legacy!" Tripp said as he helped unfold and set up more chairs. The crowd just kept growing. We had tried to find opportunities for everyone to participate in a way that felt right to them.

Many people prepared some of Carl's favorite dishes. There were deviled crabs, pimento cheese, shrimp and grits and, of course, Miss Lucy had donated a few dozen large pies and lots of her smaller ones. She seemed to have remembered everyone's favorite. There would be no need to rush today. There was plenty for everyone. Allen came back to the island and brought several gallons of his delicious sun tea. Someone else had prepared a photo album featuring many of the homes Coastal Carl had sold. Many pictures included the families that had become island residents because of his work. Neighbors talked to neighbors, remembering the one person who had connected so many in our community. With the details of the horrible way Carl's life had ended remaining right on the fringe, the day remained joyful. People were grateful for Carl and the way he had embraced this community.

As the crowd grew, the Island Croakers sang a couple of Carl's favorites, including "American Pie." This group was irreverent, quirky, and wonderfully Mongin. It was perfect for this moment. Next on the agenda was an open forum for tributes. Tripp stood up and invited the crowd to share their thoughts. Very quickly, a line formed to the right of the microphone and it was lovely to hear the funny stories, the insights, the ways Carl had affected so many people.

"Miss Carr?" A soft voice caught my attention and I turned around to see Jacob standing a few feet behind me.

"Jacob, my friend, how wonderful to see you! I would like to introduce you to my daughter, Meredith, and my son, Nicholas." I smiled at him and turned to my children. "Guys, this is one of my customers, Jacob. He just moved to Mongin Island." As I finished speaking, Buddy left my side and went to lean against Jacob's legs. I noticed Jacob scratch Buddy's head gently, using his fingers to make small circles in the black fur.

"Hi, Jacob!" Meredith greeted him warmly. He smiled shyly at her.

"Jacob, great to see you!" Nicholas said. "Looks like you already met Buddy!" Jacob beamed at him, looking like he had just been invited to sit at the big kids' table.

"Buddy is so awesome," Jacob said. "I really like him." Nicholas walked over to Jacob and crouched down next to him. They were soon absorbed into a conversation about all kinds of animals that live on Mongin, including the many deer who often were unfazed by humans and allowed you to really watch them as they meandered through the woods.

After a few minutes, Jacob approached me again. I felt he wanted to say something, but didn't have the words. I looked down at him, gently placed my hand on his shoulder and quietly said, "It's fine to tell me what you are thinking right now, if you want to. I am ready to listen if you want to share."

He surprised me by saying, "Would it be okay if I spoke too? Would it be okay if I told a story?"

"Jacob, yes! Of course! You are an island resident, you live here, you are absolutely welcome to share a story. That would be wonderful for you to do," I said, and he was gone before I could say anymore. I wanted to tell him how proud I was, how brave he was, but he was mission focused. I saw those beginning signs of a new confidence blooming in him.

When it was finally his turn, my heart melted. He looked even smaller standing in front of this crowd and I could see him biting his lip, rubbing his hands on his shorts. "I am Jacob and I live on the property, in the employee housing with my mom. My mom works here at the resort, so I didn't know Mr. Carl and he didn't sell us a house." He stopped talking and took a deep breath. Was that all he wanted us to know? Meredith had her hands poised and ready to clap for Jacob. I smiled. I guess she was also a softy, like her mom.

"I moved here a few weeks ago and didn't know anyone. I've moved a lot. We sometimes have to leave places so fast, I don't have time to pack so I came here without a lot of things. It's okay because we don't really need much. I met Miss Carr and Buddy on almost my first day here. Miss Carr told me that I would make friends with the other kids but I didn't really believe her. I don't usually have a lot of friends but I really hoped it might be true."

He continued, "Mongin Island is the first place that I have had friends. I have a home now and my mom and I are happy here. So, I just wanted to say thank you for letting us live here and for letting my mom work here. Thank you for letting us be friends. My mom is not sad every day and she told me she thinks we will be able to stay here. I am so happy about that."

While he looked at the ground, several children from the crowd had walked up and stood with him. It was the most extraordinary thing to see. These beautiful children, the next island generation, showed us all what it meant to be part of this community. Jacob needed support and they gave it. Not because someone told them to but because they understand we are people who show up for each other.

Jacob finished with: "I just want to say that I am really, really happy to finally have a real home, just like what Mr. Carl did for some of you." He handed the microphone to the next person and walked back to the pie table surrounded by his group of friends. There wasn't a dry eye in the crowd. This little boy had summed up living on Mongin Island so beautifully and simply.

As the afternoon went on, it was nice to see Theresa mingling with the Mongin Island residents. Barb turned to me and softly said, "Do you think she is looking for some leads?"

I laughed and responded, "At this point, anything is possible."

Theresa walked over to say, "Carl would have been very humbled by this if it was possible for him to be any more modest. I know you probably don't want to keep rehashing the same story, but I feel funny asking the others. I don't want to gossip, but would it bother you if I asked you just a few more questions about Paul?"

I said, "Of course, Theresa, what is it?"

She smiled and said, "I just can't figure out how Paul knew about the bodies buried at Governor's Point and well, I guess this is two questions really: what happens to those poor souls now?"

"Remember how Paul wanted these very hard-to-find nonfiction books?" I said. "Well, in a couple of these there are references to the actual burial site and apparently, there is enough of a description for

Paul to have figured it out. One book has a pretty detailed map and I think that helped narrow it down. The bodies are buried in the acreage of Governor's Point, but I still don't think he—or anyone—knows the exact location. The book is so rare that it isn't digitized, so he needed the physical text to confirm it. The officials in London who handle such claims would never have accepted his claim without the proof."

"Very interesting," Theresa said.

I said, "As far as the British soldiers' remains, I think the two governments are working it out—at least that's what we've heard on the island. Ultimately, we don't know what will happen, but I do know Scott Campino is in a holding pattern again until it's resolved. This guy can't catch a break with this land. He will have to wait for an archaeological survey to find the remains before any kinds of transactions occur. Hopefully, the British government will come to excavate, but time will tell."

"I see," Theresa said slowly. "That's really too bad because I think I've found another person interested in Governor's Point. Hmm, well I guess, time will tell. Anyway, someone Carl mentored a couple of years ago reached out to me and said he was interested in picking up where Carl left off on Mongin Island. You might be getting a new realtor here soon and who knows, maybe he will take care of the lighthouse too. His name is Adam Bledsoe and I will be driving around with him sometime next week. I will make sure to stop by your shop and introduce him."

With that Theresa smiled, turned, and disappeared into the crowd.

I turned to Barb and smiled, "So, if I ever ask you to take pictures with me—"

She threw her head back and laughed. I smiled. She shook her head as she answered, "We may be done with pictures for the time being, but I can only imagine the adventures we are going to have together. I am glad you're here, Carr. I am so glad you came home to Mongin Island."

It is my sincerest hope that you enjoyed *All Is Now Lost*—meeting some new friends like Carr, Barb and Tripp and imagining time on Mongin Island. Please share your thoughts with me by leaving a review on your bookseller's website and/or on Goodreads.com.

As part of The Island Mystery series, Carr and her friends will have more adventures on their beloved island. Stay tuned for Book 2 and please check my website for updates and the opportunity to subscribe to my insider's newsletter. All of the latest news can be found at TheIslandMysteries.com.

Thank you for sharing this journey with me!

Wishing you lots of island magic,

Laura Elizabeth